"Why did you help me today? Why did you help my daughter?"

Did Grace not remember? Draven wondered. Had the trauma wiped out the memory of what she'd wrung from him that day? He gazed into blue eyes he'd first seen looking up at him from a pile of devastation. They'd been full of pain and fear that day, but nothing could vanquish the fierce life he'd seen there.

"I promised you."

Her eyes widened, her face paled. "Oh, my God."

"You remember."

She sucked in an audible breath. "I remember everything about that day." Her gaze narrowed. "And I remember it exactly. I asked you to take care of my daughter when I…"

"Died." He said it bluntly.

"I was sure I was going to. But I didn't, so keeping that promise is unnecessary."

"The fact that you didn't die does not release me from that promise. Grace, I should have found you sooner."

Dear Reader,

Make way for spring—and room on your shelf for six must-reads from Silhouette Intimate Moments! Justine Davis bursts onto the scene with another page-turner from her miniseries REDSTONE, INCORPORATED. In *Second-Chance Hero*, a struggling single mother finds herself in danger, having to confront past demons and the man who haunts her waking dreams. Gifted storyteller Ingrid Weaver delights us with *The Angel and the Outlaw*, which begins her miniseries PAYBACK. Here, a rifle-wielding heroine does more than seek revenge—she dazzles a hot-blooded hero into joining her on her mission. Don't miss it!

Can the enemy's daughter seduce a sexy and hardened soldier? Find out in Cindy Dees's latest CHARLIE SQUAD romance, *Her Secret Agent Man*. In Frances Housden's *Stranded with a Stranger*, part of her INTERNATIONAL AFFAIRS miniseries, a determined heroine investigates her sister's murder by tackling Mount Everest and its brutal challenges. Will her charismatic guide be the key to solving this gripping mystery?

You'll get swept away by Margaret Carter's *Embracing Darkness*, about a heart-stopping vampire whose torment is falling for a woman he can't have. Will these two forbidden lovers overcome the limits of mortality—not to mention a cold-blooded killer's treachery—to be together? Newcomer Dianna Love Snell pulls no punches in *Worth Every Risk*, which features a DEA agent who discovers a beautiful stowaway on his plane. She could be trouble…or the woman he's been waiting for.

I'm thrilled to bring you six suspenseful and soul-stirring romances from these talented authors. After you enjoy this month's lineup, be sure to return for another month of unforgettable characters that face life's extraordinary odds. Only in Silhouette Intimate Moments!

Happy reading,

Patience Smith
Associate Senior Editor

Please address questions and book requests to:
Silhouette Reader Service
U.S.: 3010 Walden Ave., P.O. Box 1325, Buffalo, NY 14269
Canadian: P.O. Box 609, Fort Erie, Ont. L2A 5X3

Second-Chance Hero
JUSTINE DAVIS

Silhouette®

INTIMATE MOMENTS™

Published by Silhouette Books

America's Publisher of Contemporary Romance

SILHOUETTE BOOKS

ISBN 0-373-27421-1

SECOND-CHANCE HERO

Copyright © 2005 by Janice Davis Smith

Books by Justine Davis

JUSTINE DAVIS

lives on Puget Sound in Washington. She says that years ago, during her career in law enforcement, a young man she worked with encouraged her to try for a promotion to a position that was at the time occupied only by men. "I succeeded, became wrapped up in my new job, and that man moved away, never, I thought, to be heard from again. Ten years later he appeared out of the woods of Washington State, saying he'd never forgotten me and would I please marry him. With that history, how could I write anything but romance?"

Chapter 1

"I diverted a plane to pick you up, should be there within the hour."

Already diverted a company plane? John Draven took a deep breath before answering his boss, Josh Redstone.

"You seem awfully sure I'm going."

"I already apologized," Josh said.

He had said, not very convincingly, that he was sorry to interrupt Draven's time off. Draven had refrained from pointing out that you couldn't interrupt what hadn't yet begun.

"I'm on leave." He repeated what he'd said when Josh had first called.

"And you still will be. I just need you to do this one thing first. This is something only you can handle," Josh said.

Only he could handle? From what Josh had told him, it was a simple case of sabotage, from someone among the population of ten or so thousand who apparently didn't like the idea of Redstone coming to that unnamed little cay off the coast of Belize. Nothing any one of the team couldn't handle.

Draven felt how tightly he was gripping the phone. He frowned. Relaxed his fingers. Yet another sign, he thought. He'd always been able to separate inner tension from bodily reaction. But not now. And that was what had gotten him into this.

"Besides, when you're done with this problem at the construction site, you can stick around. Do some diving. The Belize reef is one of the best dive spots in the world."

So that was Josh's master plan, he thought. Force him to relax. Josh was big on that kind of thing, making sure his people took care of their spirits as well as their bodies.

"I know," he said.

And he couldn't deny that diving had already been on his list of things he might consider for this supposed leave of absence. He hadn't been pleasure diving in a long time. For the past several years, all his dives had been work-related, whether it was simply checking the function of an underwater system, or doing a hull check for explosives on a Redstone vessel that had been too long in port in a volatile part of the world.

The idea of days of simply drifting in the warm waters off the Central American coast held a definite appeal. Under water the world above barely existed. Down there it was peaceful, quiet and fascinating, the only predators the ones you knew on sight. Unlike that world up top, where they sometimes came in disguises so clever you didn't find out until it was too late.

Now he knew he was in trouble. He never thought of things like that. He resisted the urge to blurt it all out to his boss. But how could he tell the man who trusted him with the safety of the empire he'd built, "I nearly slugged a guy for just mouthing off?" Or "I lost control and threw a chair through a window?" Or worse yet, "I nearly blew a job and got one of our own hurt, because I couldn't keep a grip on my temper?"

"Look," Josh said, "you go, contact our people, handle what you find—no matter what it is—and then you're on your own."

That one phrase triggered Draven's radar; they knew what the problem was, so what did "no matter what it is" mean? He didn't feel capable of handling anything at the moment. He didn't even have the energy to ask for details. But he owed Josh Redstone a great deal. He also knew Josh would never trade on that, and wouldn't ask this of him unless he really thought it was necessary.

And Josh Redstone wasn't often wrong.

When he hung up and went to get his largest duffel bag, he knew he'd been manipulated. But it was Josh, so he couldn't bring himself to resent it. They'd come a long way since the day he'd shown up at a ramshackle hangar in Iowa to tell Josh his brother's dying thoughts had been of him. He'd quickly seen what Jim had meant when he'd said Josh was a dreamer, that he'd either do glorious things or nothing, but not end up in between.

Glorious had obviously been the choice. Tiny Redstone Aviation, riding on the wings of Josh's self-designed Hawk 1 jet, had quickly grown into a varied, global entity worth more than Draven could even wrap his mind around. Yet Josh Redstone was the most genuine, unassuming and generous person Draven had ever known, and he was not a man who was easily convinced of the goodness of anyone. He'd seen too much, dealt with too many of the opposite ilk.

Draven put the bag on the bed and turned to his laptop, already booted up and on his small desk. While he searched for the data he wanted online, he searched his memory for what he knew about Belize from a brief visit to Belize City years ago. Redstone had done a project or two in the area before, and he'd read the informational data. Population well under a million. Airports minimal with paved runways, and only one with a runway length of over fifteen hundred meters. The inevitable drug trade in that part of the world had a solid foothold, with the threat to grow.

But they had an abundance of natural treasures, not just the diving Josh had mentioned. Tourism was the answer to many of the country's woes, and they knew it. And were promoting it, widely. So it was easy to find out what concerned him at this moment: the weather. Eighties, he read on the Web site, this time of year. Humid. Rain frequently, usually better than six inches in July. That would get better in August, they promised.

He shut down the laptop and slipped it into the case. He put the case in the duffel bag, followed by his shaving kit, a few short-sleeved T-shirts, khakis and jeans, one lightweight jacket and, just in case he had to do any midnight recons, a set of black jeans and matching long-sleeved shirt. His hair was dark enough that he didn't worry about covering it, but it was long enough to get in his eyes, so he threw his usual knit cap in more to control it than cover it. He added a camouflage paint kit and a few other odds and ends he thought might come in handy. He did most of it without much thought; it was routine to him, and he usually had a good sense of what might be needed.

The problem with that was that it gave him too many free brain cells to think with. And as seemed typical lately, he couldn't seem to stop himself from thinking about the last thing he wanted to remember, his meeting with Josh two days ago. Draven knew he would never forget the look on the man's face when he realized what Draven had handed him was his resignation.

Draven had been face-to-face with some of the most vicious humans on the planet, and he'd felt nothing like the unease he'd felt then. He saw the moment when Josh shifted from shock and concern to determination, and when the barrage began, he'd been ready.

"Are you sick?"

Not physically. "No."

"Someone else sick?"

Josh knew there was no one else. "No."

"In legal trouble?"

If only it were that simple. "No."

"Financial?"

Redstone paid him more than he could ever imagine spending in his life. "No."

"Do you want out of the field? A desk?"

He'd go insane, locked up inside all day. "No."

Josh looked at the letter again. Read it as if the wording had somehow changed. Then he looked back at the man standing at parade rest in front of him. When he spoke again, it was in the soft voice Draven had been dreading.

"We've been together a lot of years, Johnny. You've helped me build Redstone into what it is. Don't you think I deserve a little more than 'It is with great regret I tender my resignation?'"

"Yes."

Draven's voice had been as gruff as Josh's had been soft. Nothing in his life or career had been as difficult as quitting on the man he admired most.

They'd finally compromised on this unwanted leave of absence. So as long as he wasn't officially unemployed, he was still Josh's man.

Finished packing, he slung the duffel over his shoulder. He locked the door of the small studio apartment behind him, not that there was anything of real value in it. He wasn't there enough to make him want to invest in much. Most things he personally valued were tucked away in his locker at Redstone, although none of them would matter much to anyone else. If you didn't count the shares of Redstone he owned, and the investment portfolio Harlan McClaren had built for him, the most expensive thing he owned was the laptop he'd just packed.

That and the holstered weapon at the small of his back.

He strapped the duffel on the back of his motorcycle. He'd long ago sold his last car. For the same reason as the apartment, it didn't make sense to let a car sit and depreciate when he wasn't around to drive it. The serviceable bike had enough power, was reliable and didn't have the name, chrome or flash that made it a theft target. Suited him just fine.

When he pulled through the security gate at the airfield utilized by Redstone Security for scrambling to various parts of the worldwide Redstone empire, he rode to the back of the unmarked Redstone hangar. He unlocked the small door with his code, and rolled the bike inside. He parked it in the back corner, then trotted up to the loft where the lockers were.

He didn't think he'd need heavy firepower, but given the part of the world he was headed to, and the reason, he needed something. He'd take the 17-round Glock he was wearing, and a smaller backup just in case. He added a satellite phone and a couple of boxes of ammunition, glad yet again for the convenience of not having to fly commercial.

On the thought he heard the roar of a jet engine, unusual enough at this small airfield to tell him there was a good chance it was his ride. He stepped outside just in time to see a sleek gray-and-red craft land dead center with a feather touch and nary a bounce.

His brows furrowed. This had to be it, they were the Redstone colors, but…

"Holy skyrocket," he breathed.

It was the Hawk V. It had to be. No markings, just the tail number, but the unmistakable color scheme of Redstone. And a cutting-edge design, smaller than the biggest Hawk, the recent Hawk IV that Josh personally flew, but also sleeker and more efficient. It was still in prototype stage, although two had been completed and were undergoing intense testing.

One, apparently, was about to make a test trip to Belize.

"Well, shoot, Josh," Draven said to himself with a grin, "all you had to do was say the flight was on this and we could have saved a lot of time and talk."

He went back to get his gear. By the time he locked the door behind him, the jet was coming to a halt on the apron beside the hangar. And a small fueling truck was already in sight, heading their way from the big storage tanks.

A few moments later the gangway came down, dropping out of the sleek side of the craft like some loading ramp on a futuristic spaceship. He got his second surprise when the pilot hit the steps.

"Tess?"

The petite, dark-haired woman with the pixie haircut came down grinning at Draven. "You think I'm going to give anybody else the chance to test drive this baby?"

He grinned back at her; Tess was one of the few people outside his own security team who had his complete and total trust and respect. She was the best fixed wing pilot he'd ever seen, and was almost as good with a helicopter. She'd been with Redstone even longer than he had, and had flown in and out of some of the most difficult spots on the planet, under sometimes even more difficult conditions.

Even under fire. The first time he'd flown with her, when Josh had sent her to fly Draven and Redstone point man Noah Rider out of a Colombian jungle where Rider had been exploring the possibility of opening a branch of Redstone Research and Development, utilizing the local vegetation in an effort to produce cheaper medical products. The fact that it might also stabilize the area, and perhaps give them a path other than the illegal drug trade to follow, was one of the side benefits that tended to accompany Redstone projects.

But the local insurgent guerillas had quickly decided the presence of globally known Redstone was not going to help their cause, and would quite likely hurt their drug business. Draven had seen helicopter evacs in war zones that had taken less fire than Tess had that day. But she'd kept on coming, never wavered, had held the ship rock steady as he and Rider had scrambled aboard. She'd had them out of there in seconds. Only when they'd landed safely in neighboring Brazil did they see the results; it was going to take some time to mend the bullet holes in that chopper. They all knew how lucky they'd been that they hadn't been blown out of the sky, and Draven and Rider knew who to thank that they were still alive.

When Tess had taken over the personal flying for Josh, who had reluctantly given up flying himself on business flights so he could work en route, no one had been surprised. It would take one hell of a pilot to get Josh Redstone to surrender the controls. And Tess Machado was exactly that.

Draven gestured at the plane. "So, is she all she's supposed to be?"

"And more," Tess said. "Faster, more efficient, with greater range even on some of those questionable fuels we find some places."

"Quite a résumé."

She nodded. "Josh designed it after Ian Gamble came up with a new composite material that's incredibly strong, with a higher stress point than any traditional material."

Draven lifted a brow. "You mean he didn't come up with an impossible design and then tell Ian to make it work?"

Tess laughed at his description of one of Josh's typical approaches to inspiring his people. Amazingly it worked more often than not. Draven knew that was because of the caliber of people Josh hired, and the loyalty he inspired in them, but sometimes it still amazed him.

"No, although it did require some breakthrough construction techniques. But this plane is going to bring the price down to within reach of people who never thought they'd be able to afford a private or company jet."

Draven's mouth quirked upward at one corner. Tess laughed again. "I know, I know, I sound like a promo brochure or something."

"You love what you do. That's beyond price," he said.

He knew when Tess's smile faded and her gaze narrowed that his voice really had sounded as solemn as he'd thought.

"John?" she asked quietly. She was one of the few people, even at Redstone, who ever used his first name.

He didn't respond. Instead he flicked a glance at the fuel truck. "Might want to keep an eye on that fueler. He's looking more at the plane than watching what he's doing."

For a moment longer Tess kept looking at him, making it clear she knew he was dodging her tacit inquiry.

"I'll go make sure he isn't putting avgas in," she said, and turned to walk toward the fueling truck.

The fueler shifted his attention to her, with a look of male appreciation that Draven completely understood. The kid was probably about eighteen, and Tess was…well, however old she was, he didn't really know. But twice that kid's age, anyway. But it didn't really matter. She was a very attractive woman, period.

He started up the gangway into the plane. As a prototype still unscheduled for production, the interior lacked the usual

Redstone amenities and was only roughly finished, but he'd flown in much worse. And he guessed the cockpit would already be finished with all the gadgets and controls that Josh felt were standard. First and foremost Josh was a pilot. Even if it did give his insurance agent heart palpitations when he elected himself test pilot to put some new design through its paces.

Draven wedged his duffel under one of the half-dozen standard airline seats that were temporarily bolted in place. He then headed back to confirm his earlier guess. He'd been right, the cockpit was a finished work of art, and he smiled to himself.

"Like it?"

He turned to see Tess standing there, smiling. "More important, do you?" he asked.

"He's topped himself this time," she said, gesturing at the banks of dials, screens, switches and other controls. "If something's not here, it hasn't been invented yet. Enhanced vision system so you can see through heavy weather, and at night. The latest GPS, of course, and collision avoidance system. Ground proximity warning, integrated hazard avoidance system, map displays that move as you do, you name it, it's here."

"No weapons?" he asked dryly.

She grinned. "Got a jamming device for incoming missiles, will that do?"

"I suppose it will have to," he said in mock resignation.

"Hey, we got an order from a place in Asia I can't even pronounce for a Hawk IV to serve as their Air Force One because of that jammer. And there are advancements on this new plane that the commercial aviation industry won't see for years."

"Because Josh isn't afraid to take the risks." She was as passionate about this plane as Josh himself was.

"No, he's not. Not in his work."

It was Draven's turn now; he hadn't missed the undertone in her voice. "Tess?"

"Got your gear aboard?" she asked, dodging the silent inquiry just as he had hers. He let her; he could hardly do otherwise, considering.

"Yes."

"Belt in, and I'll give you a takeoff you'll never forget."

"Mind if I sit up front?"

She looked surprised. He couldn't blame her. Usually he was busy with mission plans on a flight to a job. He didn't tell her he hadn't wanted this mission to begin with, and was trying to avoid thinking about it, he who rarely avoided anything. He'd once been told, by a well-meaning woman, that it was because he didn't care enough about anything but his work to need to avoid it, and he supposed that was true. He'd seen and done too much in this life to let down his guard that much.

"Fine," she said, gesturing to the copilot's seat.

The takeoff was all she'd promised and more. The plane was both fast and quick, two very different things when it came to small planes. It was also nimble and powerful, as she showed when she banked for a three-sixty turn and straightened out all while still climbing.

"You're lucky," she said when they leveled out. "This'll only be about a five-hour flight."

"I'm also lucky," he said, "because if I was flying commercial, I'd be headed for Houston or the East Coast to make a connection, and would get to Belize sometime tomorrow."

"I can guarantee you'll get there sooner than that," Tess said.

Thanks to the distraction of the new plane and Tess's enthusiasm for it, the flight passed quickly enough. The

Hawk V performed faultlessly, and Draven was in a more equable state of mind by the time they touched down at Goldson International Airport, where all private planes were required to land in Belize.

But he was back to being edgy again by the time he'd rounded up water transport out to the island temporarily known as Redstone Cay, where the project was being built. And after he transferred from the second boat to the third—he suspected the captains were brothers, and shared the wealth with this method—he was wishing he'd just hired a seaplane, even if it had meant waiting for a couple of hours.

What they were going to need, he thought, was their own airstrip. Then at least people could get there directly, maybe even get an exception to the rule about private planes having to go into Belize City. They could—

An airstrip.

Draven's mind slammed to a sudden stop. Josh had never said exactly what stage of building they were in, had only referred to "the Redstone Cay Resort project." Draven hadn't asked, because it didn't really matter to him, his equipment would be the same regardless, until he got on scene and assessed.

An airstrip.

It made sense. Whenever Redstone built in a hard-to-reach location, particularly an island, an airstrip was often the first thing to be built. It made getting people, supplies and equipment there so much easier that it was well worth the effort and expense. And who was their premier airstrip overseer?

But it couldn't be, could it? It was too soon, too soon after the earthquake and her hospitalization? She should still be recuperating, going through therapy and rehab. Shouldn't she?

Not the way my luck's running lately.

He groaned inwardly, nearly certain now.
An airstrip.
God help him, Grace.

Chapter 2

Grace leaned back in the office chair that tended to roll to the left. She suspected the floor in the construction trailer wasn't level, but hadn't gotten around to doing anything about it yet. She'd been too busy trying to figure out who it was who had decided they didn't want an airstrip built here.

Grace O'Conner sighed. She'd done the right thing, calling the home office for help. She could design an international airport, handle most aspects of getting it built and in a pinch fly at least a prop plane in and out of it, but this was beyond her. She didn't have the training to deal with this kind of thing, and she knew it. She'd also known that what was happening was too much for the single security guard they had had up to now. He had been hired locally, with the assumption that no more help would be needed at this early stage of the project.

But as Josh Redstone had told her when she'd made the call—it still disconcerted her that the man frequently answered his own phone—no one expected her to build the airstrip and police it, too.

Odd, she thought. She had a beautiful place to work in, great weather and the full support of the mayor of the small town down the beach a couple of miles, grandly called Matola City. He'd even thrown a welcome party for them in his own home. But while her last project had been a much welcomed airfield nearly destroyed by an act of God, this one was under attack by man. And she had no idea who.

After that act of God in Turkey, she'd spent hours buried in that pile of rubble with nothing to do but try to ignore the pain and think about dying, and what would happen to Marly, her daughter, if she did. As the pain had gotten worse and no help came, her thoughts had become crazier, and she had begun to talk out loud just to assure herself she was still alive. And she bargained with God, who, if he really had caused that earthquake, had a lot to answer for. She'd sworn never to put herself in jeopardy again if he would just let her live to take care of her daughter.

And now, every time that missing foot began to ache, she was reminded of how lucky she was to be here to feel even that phantom pain, lucky that she hadn't died under that pile of fractured brick and mortar.

The form that luck had come in still haunted her dreams, but she tried not to think about it, at least not all the time. It was done, she was alive, and grateful for it.

Wearily, she rubbed at her forehead, where a headache was beginning to build. Maybe she should have listened to them after all. Here she was, on a sparsely populated sandbar of an island off Belize, battling mosquitoes, beetles the size of Volkswagens and who knew what else, when she could be sitting at home with a glass of iced tea and a nice book to read.

Like an invalid?

Just the thought stiffened her spine.

She made herself get back to business. She wondered if what was happening was bigger than simply not wanting an airstrip built, if perhaps whoever it was simply didn't want Redstone here at all. She knew that wasn't impossible. Many people who hadn't had any firsthand experience with Redstone found it hard to believe that the company really was all it was reputed to be. Once they'd dealt with them they knew the reputation was well earned, but there were still doubters. And despite the small population, she supposed there could be at least one of those here on Redstone Cay.

Of course, she knew that what was more likely was that whatever slime controlled the local drug trade was the one behind all this. They'd warned her it was a rampant problem in this part of the world, but she'd hoped that here, on this quiet, almost isolated cay, it would be minimal.

And not for the first time she felt a qualm; one of the reservations she'd had about bringing Marly down here was just that. There had not been a drug problem with her daughter yet—that she knew about—but the fourteen year old had been teetering on the edge of real trouble long enough that Grace couldn't help wondering if it was only a matter of time.

She heard the roar of a motor, one she'd come to recognize. She got up and glanced out the window, and saw the bright orange and white cigarette-style boat coming into view from the direction of the mainland. There were only two occupants, both male, one considerably taller than the other. It looked like Jorge Nunez at the wheel, and he was gesturing in the general direction of the dock.

She went back to the desk and picked up her walkie-talkie then headed outside. She slipped her sunglasses from the top of her head to her eyes as soon as she was down the steps; she'd learned early on to protect her blue eyes from the near-equatorial sun.

She headed toward the dock, curious. She paused as someone in a hard hat waved at her from the heavy equipment enclosure. The area had been empty two days ago, but now that the rain had swept through and the weather promised to hold, the fleet of graders, backhoes, earthmovers and compactors had moved in. They'd even been, with typical Redstone efficiency, two days ahead of schedule.

And that same night they'd had their second incident of sabotage. The first, a bucket of paint tossed over gravel to be used as a base, had been minor enough they'd written it off as petty vandalism, but this one had nearly cost them a very expensive piece of machinery. Sand in the fuel tank did not make for efficient running or much longevity. If someone hadn't noticed the tiny pile of sand on top of the filler pipe, they might have started the bulldozer and ruined the engine.

It appeared someone really didn't want this job finished.

The man started toward her, and after a few steps she saw it was Nick Dwyer, the foreman of the entire project.

"Ms. O'Conner," the man said, touching a finger to the edge of his yellow helmet as they stopped a few yards from the chain-link enclosure.

"Nick," she said with a nod; she'd not seen the grizzled veteran of three of her projects yet this morning. Then, with a smile, she added, "Even after all the work we've done together, I still can't get you to call me Grace, can I?"

He smiled back. "No, ma'am. You're my boss, and it doesn't seem right."

She studied him a moment, remembering. His smile faded.

"I know," he said quietly. "Time was I didn't show you that respect."

"Time was," she answered, looking steadily at his weathered face, "you didn't know I deserved it."

The smile returned. "And that's part of the reason you do," he said. "Because you know it has to be earned. And by God, you did it with that Alaska project."

"Thanks, Nick."

She couldn't deny that airstrip at Redstone Sitka had been a problem from the beginning. Building anything in Alaska was a challenge, but building an airstrip there had its own unique problems. There was the permafrost; they'd had to move the proposed site for the strip because the original location was too poorly drained. Drainage was always a problem, but at an Alaskan site, it meant ice was mixed with the finer grained sediments, which was a recipe for disaster. The last thing she'd wanted was to lose the strip to frost heaves, slumping or anything else.

So she'd come up with an idea that involved a different kind of base and a new freeze-resistant soil stabilizing compound Ian Gamble had come up with, coupled with an interlocking surface system that could expand and contract more freely. And it had been a success. Better than five years ago and constant testing had shown it was holding up better than she'd dared hope.

Nick turned to head back to the equipment, then turned back. "Oh, tell your little girl she can have that 'dozer lesson she wanted. This afternoon, after work hours."

Grace knew she was gaping, but couldn't help it. "Lesson?"

Nick nodded. "She's been asking the guys, but they wouldn't until they cleared it with me." Then, as the obvious registered, he frowned. "You didn't know? She said you said it was okay."

It was one of those moments as a parent she hated. Did she openly catch Marly in the lie, and further alienate her? Or let her get away with this one, because at least she was showing an interest in being here?

Or an interest in being able to mow the whole thing down, she amended ruefully, admitting with reluctance that she could no longer say with certainty what would be out of the realm of possibility in her daughter's behavior.

"I'll get back to you on that," she told Nick.

She let out a sigh as Nick left and she continued her trek to the dock, where the racing boat was nearing the dock now. Just getting Marly—who at fourteen was hardly a little girl anymore, in stature or attitude—here had been a major undertaking. The fact that people traveled from all over the world to vacation in this tropical, crystalline water place hadn't made much difference in her complaining about not getting to spend the summer with her friends, although now that they were here, it was hard to tear Marly away from the beach.

And those friends were exactly why she wanted her daughter away for a while in the first place. She'd seen Marly slip further and further away from the close relationship they'd once had, and while she was willing to cede some of that distance to the process of adolescence, Marly had gone beyond just that. And Grace wasn't about to let her go any further. She could only hope she hadn't already let her go too far.

She pushed the persistent worries out of her mind, and focused on the new arrival. The man with Jorge, carrying a large duffel bag, jumped nimbly onto the dock before the boat had even come to a halt or been tied off. Jorge gave him a grin and a thumbs-up, then roared away, kicking up a wake that sprayed his former passenger from the knees down. The man didn't seem to mind, or even notice.

She noted how he moved as he walked the length of the dock toward the beach. She paid more attention to that these days, comparing her own impaired stride to those of intact people, trying to see where she might improve. But never in her life would she try to imitate this easy, powerful stride; even before she'd lost her foot she wasn't built right for that walk, it was far too masculine.

Because of her concentration on his movement, she didn't really see his face until he was much closer. When she finally shifted her gaze, her breath caught in her throat. On some level, her gut knew instantly. It clenched, sending a wave of shivering sensation through her.

Her brain took longer to process what she was seeing. It ticked off each element, from the longish, nearly black hair to the wicked scar that slashed down the left side of his rugged face. And most of all the haunting and haunted green eyes that appeared in her dreams, startling her awake with the fear that she was back in that pile of rubble, pinned, dying and alone.

She had never expected to see that face again. Had decided long ago she never wanted to. It wasn't that she wasn't grateful. Or that he was hard to look at. Her reaction had little to do with what he looked like, or the fact that when she'd first seen him she'd thought him a harshly beautiful angel come for her.

To her, this man was a creature of nightmare. Her nightmare. The nightmare that had never completely ended.

And the creature was indeed coming for her.

Despite knowing she was likely here, Draven winced inwardly at the sight of Grace at the foot of the pier. Standing there, she looked much different than when he had last seen her, pale and bruised and hooked up to machines in a hospital bed.

Standing.

It finally got through to him. She was standing there, on her own two feet. Well, one of her own, and one of Ian Gamble's; the new prosthetic foot he'd designed was rapidly becoming a marvel in medical circles, Draven knew. He'd read the data as soon as he knew she'd be getting the foot.

Made of graphite and titanium, yet incredibly flexible, it had built-in biofeedback microprocessors that could read the angle, direction and intensity of the strain put on the foot every tenth of a second. It could adjust almost as quickly as a natural foot to different walking speeds and conditions, making it much more stable than previous prostheses.

And then she started walking toward him, and he was reminded yet again just how good Ian Gamble was. It took him a moment to realize he was fixating on that to avoid the rush of awareness flooding him. She was walking, and walking easily, less than six months after the removal of her mangled foot.

He should have thought of this long before it had come to him in the plane. The same strength that had allowed her to survive three days pinned under a pile of concrete had also sped her through the rehabilitation process. He'd even known how fast it had gone, because he had requested constant updates. And the bills; he and Redstone had made certain she'd gotten the best. He marveled at the ease of her gait, noting there was barely a trace of difference between the natural foot and the prosthesis. If he hadn't known to look, he would never have seen it. Not for a while, anyway.

Of course, that could be because he was distracted by the sight of her. She'd cut her hair, and the short, wispy, windswept dark locks suited her. And bared a neck he'd never realized was so long and graceful. She was thinner after her ordeal, but when she pulled off her sunglasses, her blue eyes were just as blazingly bright and alive as they'd been when he'd uncovered her in that mound of debris.

He hadn't been at all surprised when Josh had sent the order for all available Redstone personnel in the country to respond to the small town struck hardest by the earthquake.

He hadn't been surprised when he arrived to find most of them, knowing their boss, were already on their way anyway. Nor had he been surprised when they refused to give up, digging through collapsed buildings, scouring every damaged structure in the gradually fading hope that someone else, anyone else, would be found alive.

He had been surprised to find someone alive. They'd been on the verge of turning loose the cadaver dogs when one of the searchers had sent up a shout of discovery.

He stopped the recollection with the discipline of years of training. Despite his long, hard history there were not many things John Draven dodged—or that gave him nightmares—but the memories of this woman, and what had happened to her, were at the top of his short list.

When she was close enough that he could see her expression, he realized she was startled to see him. *I know the feeling,* he thought. He wasn't, however, startled by her reaction. He was certain he was the last person on earth Grace O'Conner wanted to see again. Ever.

When they were face-to-face, she didn't speak. She just stared at him in a way that told him she was remembering, probably too clearly, their first encounter. He couldn't blame her for the look in her eyes, for the pain he saw there. He could understand the horror that was reflected in the blue depths.

What he couldn't explain was the feeling in his gut, that kicked by a mule feeling he'd once experienced in the literal sense.

"Grace," he said, not sure if he meant her name or the demeanor she'd exhibited under the most horrendous conditions.

"Mr. Draven," she answered, and he was amazed at how the formality stung.

Quickly he quashed the feeling, and took her lead. "You

weren't expecting me," he said, his tone as formal as hers had been.

"No."

The terseness of her response gave him his answer. She wanted nothing to do with him—and he couldn't blame her.

"I will stay out of your way as much as possible. I'll be gone as soon as the situation here is resolved. Can you tolerate that?"

For a moment he thought he saw puzzlement furrow her brow. But it was gone before he could be sure, and she spoke briskly. "I can tolerate anything that enables me to get my job done."

He nodded. "That's why I'm here."

"Then let's get going. You have a saboteur to find, I have an airstrip to build."

He noticed the tautness of her muscles as she lifted an arm to put her sunglasses back on. She turned with seeming ease on the rough gravel surface of the graded area, and he wondered if she was trying extra hard to show no sign of her changed body. Of course, he'd never seen her before the earthquake, so he had no way of knowing. The only thing he'd been aware of was that she did damn fine work, all of which he'd seen after the fact.

Get back on task here, Draven, he muttered to himself.

He started after her, since she appeared to be heading for the construction trailer, his own destination. He ordered himself not to watch her walking ahead of him, but then decided it wouldn't hurt, that he could give Ian a firsthand report on how one of his inventions was working under real live conditions, something the brilliant inventor—and husband of one of Draven's own top operatives—might appreciate.

Suddenly Grace stopped and turned around. For a split second he thought she might have been aware of his gaze on her, or perhaps just checking to see if he was looking. As any red-blooded male would. He guessed, despite recent events, he must still qualify, because he had to admit he'd been enjoying the view. She was wearing black jeans and a vivid blue tank top in the Belizean warmth. They weren't snug, but nothing could disguise the feminine curves.

"Are you here officially?"

It took him a moment to process, and once more he had the thought that he was not functioning at full capacity. "Officially?"

"Do you want the crews to know you're here?"

"You haven't told anyone?"

"No. I thought you might want to get the lay of the land first. Our local guy quit, after the last incident, so they know Redstone security will be coming. But that's all. They didn't know it would be John Draven."

She said it as if the announcement of his name alone would solve the situation. Which, on occasion, it had.

"Let's keep it that way for a while. I'm just the security guy they were expecting," he said. He took out a card, scribbled his cell number on it and handed it to her. "If anything happens when I'm not around," he explained, then asked, "what are the chances someone on the inside is involved?"

He liked that her response wasn't immediate but thoughtful.

"Slim. Very. Most of these people have worked for Redstone, and some of those for me, on several projects. But I never say never."

Cautious. He liked that, too. She wasn't blind. Redstone hired the best, let them do what they were hired to do, backed them up and paid them what they deserved, earning the kind of loyalty mere money couldn't buy. It was the foundation of the Redstone empire, and anyone who worked there long enough not only came to believe it, but live by it.

But every now and then a bad apple slipped through.

There had been some recently, and it had put everyone more on their guard. He wondered if, even tucked away in the hospital, she knew that, and that was why she was wary, or if it was just a natural trait. Not that it mattered, he told himself, as long as she was.

"Do you have any questions?"

She stopped and looked over her shoulder at him. "I figure you know what you're doing, or you wouldn't have the reputation you have. I'll just follow your lead."

Grace O'Conner left him standing there, and vanished into the trailer.

"Don't call me that!"

Draven's brow twitched, his only visible reaction to the young girl's angry tone and mutinous expression. He'd run into her on his first recon of the site, and had known immediately who she was.

"How'd you know my name anyway? And who I am?"

She had Grace's eyes, he thought. Her hair was a medium-brown rather than Grace's gleaming sable, and she moved with that gawkiness of adolescence rather than Grace's easy…well, grace, he thought, but the eyes were definitely the same deep blue.

"It's the name on your passport," he said mildly.

He'd seen a copy of the document in the files he'd gone over during the flight. And it was a good thing he'd guessed she was the only child on the project; she certainly didn't look anything like the smiling, cheerful child in the passport photograph. Usually it was the other way around, and it was the photo that was stiff and stern looking.

"I don't care what that thing says." She folded her arms across her chest in a message even someone who'd never heard of body language could read. "I hate that name and I won't answer to it."

"Something wrong with Marilyn?"

The girl gave an ungracious snort and rolled her eyes. "It's bad enough my mother got named after some fairy-tale-type princess, why did she listen to my grandmother's suggestion and stick me with the name of an old-time actress who killed herself?"

"I see."

He didn't, really. He didn't see or know anything about kids her age. Especially girls. They were a foreign species to him. But if she was a typical example, he was amazed any teenager survived to adulthood without being killed by their parents. His own parents had given up on him fairly early, but he'd long ago realized he probably deserved it. He'd been out of control. He'd needed more regimentation than his rather free-spirited parents had been able to provide. They'd been horrified when he'd joined the army, proud but still puzzled when he'd become a ranger, but in the end, even they had admitted it had been the saving of him.

"Ms. O'Conner, then? Or should I just say, hey, you?"

"I don't use that, either!"

He was striking out, it seemed. Which didn't surprise him, given that the only teenager he'd ever dealt with had been his cousin, who had suffered a serious case of hero-worship for the ten-years-older cousin who came home in a uniform.

"Just because my mother—" she emphasized the word with an anger that startled him "—dumped my father and his name, doesn't mean I will. I'm more loyal than that. I hate being here instead of at home with my friends, and I hate her!"

Ah. Apparently sabotage wasn't the only problem Grace was dealing with.

"'Hey, you, it is, then.'" Tired of the sparring, he turned to go. To his surprise, she called out, in a tone that seemed almost apologetic.

"I'm Marly. Marly Palmer."

He looked back over his shoulder. He gave her a slight nod, but added, "If your mother approves."

As easily as that the anger was back. "Everything's always subject to her royal approval."

"It's in the mother job description."

She scowled at him.

"And I don't envy her the job," he muttered, and turned away again.

He resisted the urge to look back at her, then wondered why he'd felt the urge at all. But he couldn't resist the idea that formed in his mind.

Did Grace's daughter want to go home so badly she'd resort to sabotage?

Chapter 3

Draven came awake instantly at the sound of what had to be at least a 500 horsepower Caterpillar motor. With that innate sense of time he'd always had, he knew he'd only been asleep an hour or so, which would put it at about midnight. Midnight, and someone had fired up a piece of equipment worth hundreds of thousands of dollars. A piece of equipment that could likely do hundreds of thousands of dollars worth of damage.

He rolled to his feet from his bedroll on the construction trailer floor. In a split second he had pulled on the slip-on boots he'd long ago gone to for just this reason, and was running. He'd already planned his route to various areas of the project, in case he had to do just this, respond in a hurry and silently.

He got within sight of the chain-link equipment enclosure just in time to see a huge piece of machinery, with a couple of fits and starts, roll through the open gate. Whatever it was, it was at least ten feet tall and thirty feet long, with a large set of wheels in front and a smaller set trailing the body in back.

Hunkered in the shadow of a wheeled bulldozer, he couldn't see into the elevated glass cab of the machine, although whoever was handling it seemed to have smoothed things out. He started to stand when he caught a movement on the ground from the corner of his eye.

There were two of them.

He reached for the gun at the small of his back and drew it out. He hadn't bothered to unclip the holster, since he wanted the weapon close at hand. Besides, he was used to sleeping with it. Or rather, dozing with it, since it also served the purpose of keeping him from getting too comfortable when he needed to be on guard. He held the lightweight Glock in his left hand. He and, at his insistence, all his people, were as skilled as possible with either hand.

Then something about the man on the ground caught his attention. He was wearing a hard hat.

Draven thought fast. What were the chances somebody from the outside bent on mischief would bring or risk stealing a hard hat? Or even think about it? For that matter, did their saboteur really think no one would notice what he—or they—were doing, starting up a machine that could be heard for hundreds of yards down the beach?

Unless they were complete idiots, they'd know the people on the site would be on guard by now. And while he couldn't discount the idiotic possibility, his gut was telling him something else was going on here. Especially since the machine was now moving smoothly, driven by someone with experience. Not that one of the people living on the cay couldn't know how to run the thing, but still…

The man on the ground moved, turned slightly as he watched the big machine roll by. And when he saw the profile Draven relaxed slightly, enough to slip the handgun back in the holster. It was foreman Nick Dwyer. Draven recognized him from the file he'd studied on the plane. He'd worked for Redstone for nearly two decades, and he was near the bottom of Draven's suspect list, and only on it at all because he had access to every part of the project.

Draven started walking, openly now. Over the noise of the big diesel Nick didn't hear him approach, so when he spoke the man jerked slightly in surprise.

"A little midnight work?"

"Oh! Oh, no, it's just…Ms. O'Conner."

Draven blinked. "What?"

Nick gestured at the machine. "She just wanted to see if she could still do it." He studied Draven for a moment. "She lost her right foot, you know. That bad earthquake in Turkey."

"I know." He didn't tell Nick he'd been there. He didn't tell anyone. It was the only job he'd ever tried to keep secret.

The man nodded. "She was very good on the loader, the compactors—well, on most of the rigs—before, but she hasn't had the chance to try since she got that new mechanical foot thing. She didn't want to try it in front of the whole crew, just in case." The man glanced at the moving machine and grinned. "But I'd say she'll do just fine."

Draven stared at the huge, yellow machine, trying to picture Grace at the controls. It was difficult if he thought only about her size and beauty, but if he remembered the toughness that had gotten her through three days buried alive, and the determination that had hurried her through rehab and back to work, it was easier.

"She's always done that?" he asked, nodding toward the machine.

"Every project I've been on with her," Nick replied. "She says she doesn't like ordering others to do things she can't or won't do herself."

"Fits," Draven said.

"Redstone? Yeah, she does. Mr. Josh got a good one there."

He'd meant more than just Redstone, meant that it fit with what he knew of her personally, but he didn't elaborate. It was clear the man already had a great deal of respect for Grace, and Draven suspected he'd find the same reaction among most people she supervised or worked for or beside.

He tried not to think about the emotions that must have been churning in her before she'd tried this, afraid Ian's miracle might not help her get this far.

But it had, and at that moment he thought he heard a yelp of joy over the sound of the humming diesel.

Grace woke up just before five, trembling. She hadn't had the dream in weeks, hadn't had the suffocating sensation jolt her awake, but it had returned last night. It wasn't hard to figure out why; the appearance of John Draven explained many things, including the recurrence of her nightmare.

Now if she could just explain the sudden leaping of her heart that seemed to occur every time she saw him. Earlier, during her self-imposed driving test, she had been able to write her reaction off to excitement at how well her new foot worked, at how quickly Ian Gamble's invention had adapted, in only a few minutes learning what feedback she needed to control the grader.

When she had whooped in victory and turned to raise a triumphant fist to Nick, and seen John Draven's unmistakable tall, lean figure standing there, she'd been startled, that's all. She hadn't known he was still on-site, had assumed he'd gone for the night.

But that didn't explain why she was relieved that he left before she turned the grader around and brought it back.

"Seems like a nice guy," was all Nick said when she asked

if that had been the security man, just to make sure she hadn't been way off in her certainty about who had joined him.

But now she'd been revisited by the nightmare she'd hoped gone forever, although the Redstone counselor had warned her some form of it would likely be with her for a very long time. Draven's presence was obviously dragging up those quashed memories, and she knew from long, sad experience that there would be no going back to sleep for a while.

She sat up and swung her legs over the side of the queen-size bed. She still wasn't quite used to the layout of the big, almost luxurious RV Redstone had set up for her use, so she turned on the low-wattage night-light.

The bedroom in the rear of the converted bus was spacious, with a slide out that did away with any feeling of being cramped. Marly had tried to negotiate for the bedroom for herself, wanting privacy with typical teenage urgency. Grace had agreed easily, with the proviso that since the bedroom had the only shower Marly mustn't complain about being awakened when her mother had to use it before dawn. That had quickly changed the girl's mind.

Now Grace was wishing she'd left well enough alone and let the girl have the room uncontested. Right now her daughter was using the foldaway bed up front, and while it was quite comfortable, it also had access to the outside door, and with Marly in her current frame of mind Grace wasn't too happy about the idea that the girl could sneak out and she'd never know.

With a sigh over the travails of single-parenting a teenage girl, Grace reached down and massaged the stub of her lower leg. It needed to toughen up more; even though she assiduously followed the doctor's instructions on keeping it dry and protected, just the nature of her work stressed flesh and machine to the max. Bless Ian Gamble for thinking about comfort as well as his amazing programming and biofeedback chip; she knew she would never have come as far as she had without the extra thought he'd given to all aspects. A true Redstone man, she thought, and gave thanks once more to Josh Redstone for seeing the brilliance beneath the absent-minded professor exterior.

She smiled slightly as she thought of what it must be like to be married to such a man, and about what had to be a very unusual relationship. Samantha and Ian Gamble were an unlikely but clearly successful pair; everyone at Redstone knew how crazy they were about each other. An inventing genius married to a highly trained and efficient Redstone security agent—

And there she was, back to Draven again. The security team was his creation, most said it was his life, and some said it was also his soul.

Trying to shake off thoughts of the man who haunted her nights but whom she thanked by day, she stood up. She reached for the crutch she used at night from where it leaned against the nightstand. She could hop to the bathroom, but in an RV, even a well-built one like this, it tended to make enough vibration to wake Marly up.

She splashed some water on her face, as if that would wash away the remnants of the dream. She knew better, but at least she felt as if she was doing something.

She would look in on Marly, she decided. Then she'd just get dressed for work. She was due in about an hour anyway, and she could always find something to catch up on.

"Catch up, what a concept," she muttered to herself as she went to the door between the bedroom and the rest of the motor home and pulled it carefully and quietly open.

A moment later she was through the door and standing beside the converted sofa, her heart hammering as what she'd feared since they'd arrived greeted her.

Her daughter was gone.

Chapter 4

She knew Marly had made it to bed. She didn't go to sleep herself until the girl was tucked in for the night. Marly told her it was childish, and Grace had managed to disconcert her by telling her that her mother had the right to be childish if she wanted to be.

She leaned down and felt the bedding. Cool. Well, as cool as it ever was in this tropical climate. But while the pillow held the impression of Marly's head, there was no body warmth left. And the clothing she'd had on earlier was gone, instead of tossed on the floor in the girl's usual manner. There was no way to know when she'd left. Nor did it matter. What was important now was finding out where her daughter was.

And when she's back, I'm going to read her the riot act about scaring me like this, Grace promised herself. She didn't know how much more of this she could take. It had to stop. But nothing she'd tried so far had had much effect, and she was nearly out of ideas.

She grabbed the cordless telephone, got balanced on her crutch, then hastened back to her room to dress while she made some calls.

Draven didn't think he was imagining the flurry of unusual activity. A construction site was always a busy place, but there was something else going on here. Something different than the usual routine this early in the morning. He watched the various people scurrying around, noticed the pattern of the activity and saw who was pointedly absent.

When he was sure, he headed for the equipment enclosure to find Nick.

"What's missing?" he asked without preamble.

Nick frowned, then the expression cleared. "You mean who. You didn't hear yet, I guess. Ms. O'Conner's little girl is gone."

"Marly?"

Nick gave him a curious look. "You met her, then?"

"Briefly," Draven said, his tone wry.

Nick grinned. "'Bout all most of us can take. She's been giving her mom a real hard time. But we all think an awful lot of Ms. O'Conner, so we're looking."

And that, Draven thought, said it all. Then, like throwing a switch, he clicked into investigation mode.

"She have any ideas?"

Nick shook his head. "They haven't been here that long, so she doesn't know where the girl might go. Lots of places to hide out and not be found on this island, if that's what you want to do."

"Any sign it was involuntary?"

The man looked startled. "You mean…kidnapped? No! Nothing like that. Not here. Why, they only have a part-time cop, or constable, whatever they call it, because they don't have any crime."

Draven thought of the reason he was here; they had some crime now. "Until now."

The man blinked as it registered. "Yeah. I guess." Nick gave Draven a sideways look. "I suppose given your job, you have to think that way. I mean about kidnapping and such."

Draven gave a half shrug in answer.

Nick shook his head. "I wouldn't like that much."

Sometimes neither do I, Draven thought. But right now there were more questions to ask.

"When was she last seen?"

"Last night," Nick said, "around one-thirty, when Ms. O'Conner went back after trying the grader. The girl was there then."

"Discovered gone when?"

"Around five, when she got up."

Early riser, Draven thought. Of course, on a construction project, most people were.

"What's been searched?"

"We've covered most of the site," Nick said. "Don't know where to go from here."

"The beach," Draven said, not putting into words the ugly possibilities there.

"Okay."

"Higher ground, too. Sometimes people want to see what they can see."

"Yeah, good," Nick said, his mood clearly lightening now that there was a plan of sorts.

"Any vehicles missing?" Draven asked.

Nick looked startled. "Don't know, but I'll check. You think she'd take one of the pickups? She doesn't have a license yet. I don't think she's old enough."

"If she's the type who'd take a vehicle, no license wouldn't stop her."

"Good point," Nick said with a grimace. "I'll check for anything missing."

Draven nodded. "The inflatable," he said, referring to the gray Zodiac runabout they used for supply runs to the mainland. "Make sure it's still at the dock."

"Didn't think of that, either," Nick said, eyeing Draven with even more respect.

"Where is…Ms. O'Conner?"

"Went into town, to look."

Draven nodded. When the man had gone, he walked back to the construction trailer, thinking all the way. He'd been involved with missing persons before. Often, in fact. When the son of the Redstone Human Resources director had vanished, Josh hadn't hesitated to call up the troops. It was part of working for Redstone.

That one had ended happily, with the child being found safe, but others hadn't. Reeve Fox, one of his best agents, had been on a leave of absence for nearly a year because they hadn't found one in time. She'd found the body in pieces strewn across a garage floor, and simply hadn't been able to deal with the brutality of it.

Of course, he thought as he went up the steps into the trailer, he hadn't been asked to help with the missing girl. But Grace was part of Redstone, and Redstone took care of its own. Josh would expect—and accept—no less.

Grace disconnected her call and put her cell phone back in her purse. She'd contacted Nick to tell him to call off the search, that Marly had been found. Safe, thank heavens, although the sound part was questionable just now, after what she'd been told.

She continued on her way to pick up her wayward daughter. Moments later she arrived at the town center office she'd been in once before, a holdover from the colonial days when

Belize had been British Honduras. She went straight to the office of Mayor Colin Remington, who sometimes also seemed like a holdover from those days. He had been delighted that Redstone was coming to his little island. She couldn't blame him, Redstone was welcomed almost everywhere they went.

Now the mayor had tactfully excused himself so she could speak to the other man in the room, although at the moment she was speechless, unable to quite believe what she'd heard.

"She what?" she finally managed to say.

"I'm afraid it's true," the man in the wrinkled uniform said with apparent reluctance, gesturing at the spread of makeup, perfume, magazines and candy on the desk.

Grace was stunned, and just stared at the man for another long moment. Thin, bowed, very tanned legs emerged from the khaki-colored shorts that were a concession to the tropical climate. Above the left breast pocket of the matching shirt there was a small brass tag, slightly crooked, that proclaimed him M. Espinoza.

Espinoza cleared his throat and said, "I'm sure it's just a misunderstanding, that she meant to pay."

Grace wheeled around and looked at her daughter. "You stole all this?"

The girl glared back at her. "What of it? They weren't worth buying. They don't have any good stuff here in bumbleville."

Anger spiked through Grace, and she reined it in with an effort. "I have put up with your moods, your rudeness, your sullenness and your temper. I've put up with your self-involved, it's-all-about-me attitude. But I will *not* tolerate stealing, sneakiness and arrogance."

Marly's smirk vanished.

"There are some forms to be done," Officer Espinoza— or sergeant, apparently, judging by the three striped chevrons on his sleeves—said quickly, before the girl could respond.

"Fine," Grace said, and quickly sat down in the chair the man indicated. She wondered if she should sit on her hands before she could grab her child and shake her silly. She simply could not allow that attitude to continue. Her daughter might not like her right now, but she *would* respect her.

She just wasn't sure how to make that happen.

With a sigh she picked up the papers, wondering how they'd gotten to this state. They'd always been so close, Marly had always confided in her, but now—

When the door to the office opened, Grace looked up, expecting to see the mayor coming back, with the ever-present smile of a man happy to be living in paradise. Instead her breath jammed in her throat as John Draven walked in.

Nick must have told him, she thought. But why was he here?

Draven took over the room as surely as if he were a foot taller than his already solid six feet. Even Espinoza straightened up, looking at the newcomer warily, as if sensing something that told him this was a man to pay attention to.

Or be on guard around.

The words echoed in her head, and she didn't know why she'd thought them. She caught herself gaping, and quickly lowered her eyes. She wound up focusing on his feet, but couldn't seem to stop herself from scanning upward. He wore a pair of faded jeans over boots with what looked like a crepe sole. For skulking around, she supposed. The jeans were snug, but not tight, and tucked into them was a tan T-shirt with the sleeves ripped out, baring tanned, leanly muscled arms. His chest seemed impossibly broad to her beneath the knit fabric. The overall impression was one of leashed power, and she didn't think she was alone in that assessment; Espinoza was practically standing at attention now. Clearly she wasn't the only one being affected by the sheer power of John Draven's presence.

She flicked a glance at Marly, who looked more wary than anything as she frowned as if trying to figure out why Draven was here. And with her recently developed self-centeredness, how it was going to affect her.

Exactly my question, she thought as he spoke to Espinoza first.

"Sergeant," he said, holding out a hand that the man took rather gingerly. "I'm Redstone security. I'm hoping I can help with this situation."

She noted he was speaking genially, unlike the brisk, businesslike tone she usually heard from him. She also noted he didn't give his name. She knew Redstone security preferred a low profile, and could see the reasons for it, but she hadn't realized they even tried to keep their names quiet.

"Excellent!" Espinoza appeared vastly relieved to be able to hand this over to someone other than her; male chauvinism was apparently alive and well in this part of the world. And Draven obviously knew it.

"With your help, I'm sure we can wind this up and keep Miss O'Conner out of any further trouble."

"Mr. Ayuso, he is willing to not press charges if he gets his property back and I can assure him the child will be properly dealt with. Children, they need discipline."

"That they do," Draven said, almost cheerfully. "I needed it so much I joined the army."

Espinoza laughed. Grace was in no mood for all this male bonding, however fascinating she might find it under other circumstances. She flicked a glance at Marly, who looked both wary and disgusted, no doubt because she didn't like being referred to as a child.

"I've signed these," Grace said, inserting herself back into the process. To heck with male chauvinism, *she* was Marly's mother. "What else do I need to do?"

Espinoza seemed to ponder her question.

"I'm sure there will be some sort of appropriate punishment," Draven said, although he was still looking at Espinoza, not at her, or Marly. "It wouldn't be right to just let this slide."

Espinoza suddenly grinned, and she wondered what on earth Draven had done that she couldn't see. The sergeant nodded in almost fierce agreement.

"We could put her in our cell," he said, "but I confess, it's not a nice place. The local wildlife has no trouble getting in. You know, iguanas, boas, rhino beetles and the like."

Marly sucked in an audible breath at that.

Grace was fairly certain Espinoza was staging this for Marly's benefit. What part Draven was playing, she didn't know. But because it was working she kept silent, as if she were considering that cell.

Her daughter stared at her, looking astounded. "Mom?"

Grace steeled herself against the shock in her daughter's voice. "Any other options?" she asked after a moment.

"I suppose," Espinoza said thoughtfully, looking at her now, "we could consider house arrest." He lifted a grizzled brow at her. "You have a house?"

Her mouth quirked slightly. She quashed it; she didn't want Marly to think she found anything about this even slightly amusing. "It's on wheels, but yes."

"But you are a very busy woman," he said. "Who will make certain that she stays where she's supposed to?"

She guessed things like monitoring bracelets hadn't made their way out here yet. She grimaced inwardly; they likely hadn't been *needed* before. Until her recalcitrant daughter had arrived to disrupt their little paradise.

"Her father could be involved, perhaps?"

Grace stifled a bitter chuckle. "Not likely."

Marly made a tiny sound, one that tore at Grace's heart, and she didn't dare look at her daughter's face. She knew what she would see there, and she couldn't bear it just now. Not on top of everything else. And again she thought of a special place in hell for heartless fathers like her ex-husband.

"She can be secured at our job site," Draven said.

Espinoza turned back to him. The man seemed very relieved to simply hand things over to Draven. She imagined it was an effect he found very useful on occasion. She wasn't sure she didn't feel just that way herself.

"You will be responsible for her?" Espinoza asked eagerly.

"No." Draven turned then, looking at Marly straight on. When he spoke, his voice was frosty enough to cool even Marly's temper. "She'll be responsible to me."

The girl's eyes widened. For a moment she simply stared at the man towering over her. Then she looked at Grace.

"Mom!" She yelped it this time, a near-desperate tone in her voice.

"If you wanted her help," he said, his voice softer but no warmer, "you should have rethought the way you've been treating her."

Grace stiffened. What did he know about it?

Marly started a retort, then stopped. Finally she just muttered, "I don't have to listen to you."

"Your decision. But actions have reactions. Decisions have consequences. About time you learned."

He was back to his curt, concise sentences, and Grace suddenly saw why he did it. In part, anyway. Marly had opened her mouth to protest, but closed it again the moment he spoke in that clipped tone. Once she was silent, he turned back to the sergeant, who appeared fascinated by what was happening. As, she confessed to herself, was she. She decided then to just let this play out. Perhaps a new element added to the mix might produce better results than she'd had so far.

"What else?" Draven asked Espinoza.

"Restitution to Mr. Ayuso, the store owner would be first."

"I'll take care of that right now," Grace said, reaching for her purse.

"No."

Draven's tone was sharp. Her hand stopped and her head snapped around, her gaze narrowing as she looked at him. "What?"

"Marly will pay it back herself."

"I don't have that kind of money," Marly yelped. "If I did I would've bought the stuff in the first place."

Draven just looked at the girl. "Would you have?"

Marly lowered her eyes, and Grace knew lack of money wasn't the reason for this. Her hand fell back to her side.

"You'll work for the money. We'll decide later what you'll do and how much you'll be paid. You'll bring the money to Mr. Ayuso yourself. In installments. Minimum of once a week."

"How'm I supposed to do that?"

"How did you get here today?"

"I walked." Realization widened Marly's eyes. "You can't expect me to *walk* here every week!"

"You did today."

Outrage made the girl sputter. Grace wasn't sure how she felt about it herself; it was one thing for her to be upset with her own daughter, and something else entirely for this man to be so hard-nosed with her. She was Marly's mother, she should have the final say. But he had the girl's attention, which was more than she'd been able to accomplish recently. And that had to be the bottom line, more than who did it. So she kept silent, hoping she wasn't making the wrong choice.

Things happened quickly after that. She signed some papers, trying not to let her eyes tear up as she realized that but for the kindness of a shop owner she'd met only once, her daughter would have had a criminal record. Then she accepted a copy of the list of the stolen items, showing a total cost that surprised her until she realized the prices no doubt reflected the complications of getting products out here—or the prices of the Nunez brothers, she amended wryly.

She also asked for and got the phone number for Mr. Ayuso, although Espinoza reminded her that while cellular service on the cay was good because of the new tower that had been built, landline phone service was unreliable.

"Redstone will be upgrading that," Draven said.

Espinoza gave him a wry look. "That will be good for your facility, but I doubt it will help Mr. Ayuso."

Draven smiled. Grace realized she'd never actually seen him smile before. It was charming, and pure Redstone munificence. It also made her heart do that crazy leap again.

"I meant for the whole island."

Espinoza blinked. "The whole island?"

"New system, from the ground up. Underwater cable from the mainland."

Espinoza's jaw dropped. "But why would you do that?"

"Because Redstone believes in improving the lives of those who welcome us."

"The golden touch balanced by the golden rule," Grace said, quoting the motto the media had hung on Josh Redstone long ago. It had been mocking then, but over the years he'd shown by undeniable example that it fit.

"St. Josh," Marly muttered.

Draven spun around to face her so quickly that Grace jumped and Marly gasped.

"Not. Another. Word."

His voice had gone from cold to icy. Grace couldn't see his expression, but if Marly's widened eyes and sudden paleness were a reflection of it, she was probably better off. Again she felt the urge to leap to her little girl's defense. But she'd nearly snapped at her daughter herself for her words and tone when Josh Redstone had done nothing but help them.

Marly looked at her, eyes full of pleading and indignation. The pleading made her waver, but the indignation when she was so clearly in the wrong, here and in the whole situation, decided her. She'd let Draven play this out. Her tactics of patience and indulgence certainly hadn't been working.

"Let's go," she said.

Draven kept looking at the girl. "Perhaps she should walk back. Get used to it."

"No," Grace said. "I want her within my sight for the foreseeable future."

His gaze flicked to her then, and she thought she saw a glint of approval there.

"Good point," he acknowledged. "With who?"

Grace didn't miss the change in his voice. He was asking much more than a simple logistical question. She answered the unspoken query.

"You. You heard Sergeant Espinoza. You're in charge."

Marly made a tiny movement, but she kept her mouth shut. That alone gave Grace the strength to hold steady when her daughter looked at her as if she'd betrayed her.

"I will always, always love you," she said softly, "but right now you're not very likable."

Marly lowered her gaze, and Grace's stomach knotted.

By the time they got back to the site, Grace had worked herself into quite a state wondering if she had just made the biggest mistake of her daughter's life. But she soon had a distraction.

They'd been hit again.

Chapter 5

Grace walked out onto the pier, looking down into the crystalline water. Marly walked beside her, also watching. They stopped a few feet short of where Draven and Nick were in deep discussion. Although she was glad the girl had trailed along automatically to the site of all the activity, so that she could keep an eye on her, she didn't want her overhearing anything that might frighten her. So far she'd managed to keep her worries about the sabotage from the girl, passing it off as just local mischief, and she'd like to keep it that way as long as possible.

She peered into the water. It was hard to judge how far down the Zodiac was, but she knew it had to be at least twenty feet deep here where it had been slightly dredged, because a couple of the small cargo boats that had pulled in here drew at least seven or eight feet and had been able to dock at low tide.

She looked up to ask Nick what had happened. At that

moment a movement caught her eye and when she looked, coherent thought fled.

Draven had kicked off his boots and peeled off his shirt. She knew she was gaping at him, but couldn't stop herself. It took her a moment to get past the muscular, ribbed perfection of structure and notice the collection of scars that marked the tanned skin.

"Wow," Marly said, her first words since they'd left town. "He's buff, but, man, he's beat up."

"Yes," Grace agreed absently.

Since he wasn't even glancing their way she continued to stare as he walked to the edge of the pier at the spot where the Zodiac had been tied up. She'd never been so aware before of how a man was put together. Perhaps, she thought, because she'd never seen one put together so well before.

Stop it! she ordered herself. She couldn't believe she'd even thought that.

He dove into the water in a clean, controlled arc that barely sent up a splash.

"That'd win a dive meet," Marly said; apparently Draven was no longer—or wasn't yet—on her most-hated list.

He went straight down to the inflatable, his image oscillating along with the boat's as the water rippled. He swam around it, checked the outboard motor that was half buried in the soft bottom, touched the side tubes in several places. Once he even dug into the sandy seabed, to see the bottom of one of the tubes. Then he checked the mooring line, hand-over-handing the length of it until he reached the end.

"Damn, how long can that boy hold his breath anyway?"

Grace heard Nick's exclamation, which voiced what she'd just been wondering herself. But finally, with the bitter end of the mooring line still in his hand, he headed back up.

When he broke the surface, Grace expected to hear an explosive gasp for breath. Instead it seemed as if he were barely breathing hard. Without even a pause he tossed the rope up to Nick. As Draven slicked back his wet hair, Grace glanced toward the ladder that went from the water to the deck of the pier, some twenty feet behind them, where Draven would have to go to get out, or swim the hundred feet to the beach.

When she turned back, he was already on the pier.

Marly said a word Grace would normally have chastised her for. "Did you see that?"

"No, I didn't," she admitted, forgoing the motherly instruction for the moment.

"He came up out of that water like a dolphin, high enough to grab the edge of the pier. And just *pulled* himself up like it was nothing!"

"Stay here, please," she told her daughter, and headed off the instant protest with a simple glance toward Draven.

Great, she thought. *I finally find somebody who can control her, and it has to be him.*

She buried her emotions as she joined the others, and asked briskly, "What happened to it?"

"Very large, very sharp knife."

"Reparable?"

"More than it's worth," Draven said with a shake of his head.

The movement drew her eyes to the water streaming off the dark strands of hair and over that body that had taken her breath away. Up close the scars were even more prominent, a long, heavy, puckered mark across his belly, a round indentation that she recognized as probably a bullet hole and a thin one down his left arm that looked like the one on his face. She'd seen a worker sliced by a sharp blade once, and the scar had looked like that. A knife fight?

She shuddered, and with an effort yanked her unruly mind back to the matter at hand. "Did anyone see anything?"

Nick shook his head. "Not a thing."

"Probably came underwater," Draven said.

"So we don't know when, either," she said.

"No," Nick said. "We don't know how long it's been down there. Nobody even noticed it missing until he—" he gestured at Draven "—told me to check on it."

"You told him to check on the inflatable?" she asked.

He nodded, flicking a quick glance at Marly, telling Grace just what Draven had suspected, that her daughter might have taken the boat. The thought of what could have happened if she had, with her very limited experience with boats, made Grace's stomach churn. It could have been Marly's lifeless body he'd gone into the water for.

She suppressed a shudder. With a tactfulness that surprised her, he began to issue instructions to Nick, giving her a chance to recover her composure.

"Search the site for the weapon. Any wet clothes stashed. I'll head that way." He gestured up the beach.

Nick nodded. "Think maybe he went into the water up there?"

"Too visible the other way."

She saw what he meant; the brush was heavy there, providing lots of cover. To the south was mostly open sand, with the vegetation far enough back from the waterline to make it hard to get out there without being spotted.

Draven reached for his boots, started to pull one on, then obviously realized his still-wet feet were going to be a problem. He grabbed his T-shirt off the pier and used it to dry his feet. And only then did Grace see what had been covered by the shirt: a deadly looking handgun in a holster with a belt clip lay on the boards of the pier.

Even as she stared at it, he picked it up and clipped it on

the back of his wet jeans. She realized how long she must have been gaping by the fact that he'd gotten his boots back on and she hadn't even realized it.

She watched him head up the beach, walking as smoothly on the sand as on a paved road. She shouldn't have been surprised about the gun, she realized. Of course the head of Redstone Security would be armed. Probably at all times.

Probably the first time she'd ever seen him, her harsh angel had been carrying a gun.

Too bad there hadn't been anyone or anything to shoot, she thought. *Just an earthquake. A natural disaster.*

And a very personal one for her.

Draven saw the light still on in the construction trailer when he got back to the site just after 10:00 p.m. He'd found a spot north of the pier where the brush had looked trampled, but nothing else. After that, he'd gone into town and engaged in casual conversation with a few people, slipping in some low-key questions and getting some interesting answers. With some thinking to do, he headed back to the site.

He went up the steps and pushed the door open, not expecting anything untoward because the light was on at this hour, but his hand on the butt of the Glock nevertheless.

Grace was sitting at the desk she used, and it was her light that was on. She had some design drawings spread out in front of her, and something labeled Wind Study, but she wasn't looking at any of them. In the split second before she heard him and turned around, he'd seen her slumped shoulders and her head cradled in her hands.

A sudden, aching feeling flooded him. It was unfamiliar to him, and when he finally recognized it as the need to comfort, he was stunned.

"It will be all right." The words were out before he'd even realized they were coming.

"Marly will be," she said, obviously not realizing the momentousness of what had just happened. "She's a good kid at heart, she's just having a tough go right now."

"Teenager," he said succinctly, and was rewarded with a slightly wobbly smile.

"Yes, but with her it's more than just that." She jammed her fingers through her hair. It should have messed it up, he thought, but instead it just seemed to make it more sexily tousled.

Sexily?

His own startling thought ricocheted around in his mind, and he could almost feel it chewing its way through neurons long inactive.

Damn.

Hastily he spoke again, hoping her answer would give him time to reel in that unwanted, unwelcome and poorly timed thought.

"More?"

Grace sighed. "That bit about her father, in the mayor's office?"

"I heard."

"We went that route once. Marly was angry because I wouldn't let her...I forget, do something that her friends were doing. She said she wanted to go live with him, even though he hadn't even talked to her in months. I said, 'Fine, call him.' She did."

"He didn't want her," Draven said softly.

"No. And he told her so, very bluntly. She never told me exactly what he said, but it was something about why would he want to ruin his lovely new life by having a brat around." She sighed again. "I still feel guilty over that one."

That made no sense to him. "You?"

"I had a pretty good idea what he'd say. I should never

have let her ask him. I knew she'd be hurt. I guess I just got tired of her yelling about how much better her life would be if she lived with her father."

"Some fantasies need to be ended." He thought about the name he'd seen on the passport, the name he assumed was her father's. "You can't live in them."

She leaned back in her chair and looked up at him. She seemed to be studying him with a new intensity. "I expected you to say something simple like 'She'll get over it.'"

"She will."

She rolled the pen she held between her fingers. It seemed a nervous gesture in a woman who projected such calm.

"I never had the chance to thank you for your help today," she said finally.

"Not necessary."

Her mouth quirked. "You are the proverbial man of few words, aren't you?"

He lifted one shoulder in a half shrug.

"It bothers you?" He knew his brusqueness bothered some, was misinterpreted by others, but the people whose opinion mattered understood it was just his way.

"No," she said. "It's really rather efficient."

He blinked. That was a new one. Of all the comments, gibes and observations he'd ever gotten on the subject, there had never been one that was actually a compliment.

"Besides, I know you *can* speak in full sentences. I've heard you."

He smothered the beginnings of a smile. "Yes, ma'am. Even went to college."

"Now there are some term papers I'd like to read," she said, startling him once again.

"Tossed them," he said, the image of her reading that long-ago work rattling him in ways he didn't fully understand. "Profs and I were rarely on the same planet."

She grinned at that, and that he'd managed that warmed him far too much. "I can imagine."

He walked over to the corner of the trailer and pulled out his bedroll. She glanced at the small bundle, then at him, brows furrowed.

"You're sleeping here?" she asked.

He nodded. "It's easier."

"I'll finish up quickly, then."

"Don't rush." He pulled out the spare chair beside her desk, reversed it and sat, crossing his arms over the back. "Working late?"

"Just going over some things. I had to spend some time with the mayor this afternoon, showing him around, so I'm a little behind."

"On what?"

"Inventory, mostly. I need to be sure we have all the supplies and equipment we need, since without the inflatable there won't be any quick runs to the mainland, or over to San Pedro on Ambergris Cay. Frankly, Jorge Nunez charges too much to use that speedboat of his."

"Not a problem."

"What?"

"Josh is sending a replacement inflatable and motor, plus a backup."

"He is?" she asked.

"Should be here by tomorrow."

"Oh."

She was silent for a moment, and he wondered if she was bothered by being cut out of that transaction.

"Didn't mean to step on any toes. I was already on with him, so I asked."

She blinked. "What? Oh, no, I wasn't thinking about that. I should have asked myself, I guess. But I was feeling responsible for the thing being destroyed."

"Josh doesn't work that way."

"I know. But I still felt I should have stopped it somehow."

"You're not responsible for everything and everyone. Just getting this field built."

"And my daughter."

"Yes."

She seemed to hesitate, then spoke again, lowering her gaze as if she couldn't look at him when she asked her next question.

"Why did you help today?"

"You're Redstone."

"Yes. But Marly isn't. Why did you help her?"

"She'd argue that I didn't."

A smile flickered again, but she wouldn't be distracted. "Yes, she would. Why?"

Did she not remember? he wondered. Had the trauma wiped out the memory of what she'd wrung from him that day? Should he say something generic, to avoid reminding her of it? Should he lie by omission?

He gazed down into blue eyes he'd first seen looking up at him from a pile of devastation. They'd been full of pain and fear that day, but nothing could vanquish the fierce life he'd seen there. And he knew he couldn't lie, even by omission.

"I promised you."

Her eyes widened, her face paled and she dropped the pen onto her desk. "Oh, my God."

"You remember."

She sucked in an audible breath. "I remember everything about that day." Her gaze narrowed. "And I remember it exactly. I asked you to take care of my daughter when I…"

"Died." He said it bluntly.

"I was sure I was going to."

"I know."

"But I didn't."

"No."

"Thanks to you."

He grimaced. "At great cost to you."

She shook her head as if that were negligible.

"But I didn't die, so keeping that promise is unnecessary."

The twitch of his mouth got through that time.

"The fact that you did not die does not release me from that promise."

She blinked. "Wow. When you do the complete sentence thing, you don't mess around."

He wanted to grin, but was fairly certain it was inappropriate for the seriousness of the subject. "I understand that you don't like me, of all people, being responsible for your child. And I understand why you feel that way, after…what I did that day."

"That building was about to come down and you knew it. It *did* come down, barely two minutes after you pulled me out."

"Most of you," he said tightly.

"So that's it," she said, as if in sudden understanding.

"I should have found you sooner, would have had more time to get you out."

"You did what you could." Her eyes darkened. "I won't say that I don't have awful memories. Or that seeing you doesn't bring them all back."

Draven felt his stomach clench as she put what he'd known had to be true into words. But he appreciated her honesty.

"I'll stay out of your sight whenever possible."

"Fine. I'll manage, then."

He let out a breath he hadn't been aware of holding. He didn't understand, had never understood, why this one had gotten to him. He'd splinted bloody broken bones, picked debris out of an exposed brain, cut bullets out of living flesh. All in conditions as bad as or worse than the aftermath of an earthquake.

But it was this one that haunted him. It had been bloody, long and agonizing. And she'd stood it better than most. She'd lain there, trapped in that debris, and barely let out a moan.

Even while he was sawing off her foot with a field knife.

Chapter 6

Draven took a long pull on the cold beer, having to admit to himself that it somehow tasted better, sitting at this outdoor bar surrounded by tropical plants. He didn't drink much, and when he did it was usually in circumstances like this, where there was a greater goal to his drinking.

The bartender was making something for a local, a drink that seemed to consist mainly of several varieties of rum and a tiny splash of some thick red substance whose identity he didn't want to hazard a guess at. The man took it and wandered back to the table where his friends were gathered. Draven wondered if he'd be able to walk when he finished the thing.

This was the only tavern on the island, so eventually about half the population came through. He saw some that already looked familiar, including Mr. Ayuso from the store where Marly had started her criminal career.

"Quiet place," he said when the bartender came back.

"Come on Saturday nights," the man said, flashing a smile that showed two gold-trimmed teeth. The national flag proudly displayed behind the bar told Draven he was likely from bordering Guatemala, the country that still claimed Belize as its own.

Draven smiled back. "Sometimes quiet's nice."

The man nodded, and went back to drying the glasses he had lined up on the varnished surface.

"Saw your mayor out for a walk," Draven said.

"He likes to be seen," the bartender said neutrally.

Draven gave him a grin that told him he understood the subtext. "He was complaining about some guy he called *el mercader.*"

The man's hands stilled. "The merchant. Yes."

And people react just like that when you mention him, Draven thought.

"So," he said in a buddy-to-buddy tone he'd developed long ago, "is he really as bad a guy as Mayor Remington made out? A big drug dealer?"

The man glanced around, then stared at Draven for a moment, as if to assess how much it was safe to tell him.

"You are from the Redstone people?"

He nodded.

"They are doing good things here. My business will be much better."

"That's generally how it happens, yes."

The man went back to drying his glassware. "Let us just say that if a person in Belize City wants something…stronger than what I sell here, that person would likely go to *el mercader.*"

"I feel sorry for Sergeant Espinoza, then. The mayor seemed to be riding him pretty hard."

The man frowned for a moment at the idiom.

"Pushing him to do something," Draven clarified.

"Ah. Yes, it is true. But Miguel Espinoza, he is not a fool.

He does what he must, but he knows it could mean his life to go up against *el mercader* alone."

Or was he reluctant to push because he knew someone else was responsible? Draven wondered. *Perhaps even Espinoza himself? Being the law made a great cover.*

"Besides," the bartender added, *"el mercader,* he never does business here on the cay, where he lives."

"Does he live here in town?"

"Oh, no," the bartender said, clearly grateful for that fact. "He lives on the far end of the island, in what they call the lap of luxury, I think? In the house his father built. And his home, it is very well guarded.

"His father?"

The man nodded. "He is the son, you see, of the original *el mercader.* His father was even more feared. Very brutal. Some of us even thought the son might change the business to something…"

"Legitimate?"

"Yes. That's the word. He went away to school in the United States, and when he came back there were many arguments between he and his father. So we had hope. But it came to nothing."

Draven changed to inconsequential topics as he finished his beer, then tipped the man nicely but not so much as to make it seem as if he were paying for the information. He wanted it to appear as if he'd had only normal curiosity about the local drug dealer.

He walked back to the edge of the small town thoughtfully. Mayor Remington's theory was indeed the most logical, that *el mercader* was behind the sabotage at the airstrip site. Obviously anyone in his particular line of work wouldn't be happy about the coming of radar and flight plans, and the other equipment that comes with a modern airfield. It would make sense that he try to stop it.

Draven reached the edge of town, and continued on several more yards. Once out of sight of any buildings, he glanced around to be certain no one was showing any interest in him. Then he pulled off his shirt and tucked it into the back of his jeans, arranging it to cover the Glock.

Then he ran the two miles back to the site at a blistering pace. When he got there, he added the length of the beach, pushing himself even harder on the soft sand. He stopped at last, jogged a bit to cool down. Then he peeled down to the trunks he'd worn underneath his jeans and took a plunge in the water, never getting too far from his clothes and the weapon they covered, up on the beach. Feeling loose and warmed up, he grabbed his clothes and headed back to the site to track down his new charge.

"I'm tired," Marly whined.

"Hmm."

The girl tried again. "It's hot."

"Yes."

"I want to go swimming."

"When you're done."

"I can't finish this in one day!"

Marly's voice was escalating, and Grace had to smother a chuckle as she watched from out of sight. She found Draven's verbal style amusing, and as she'd said, efficient, but it was driving the teenager crazy.

"Your choice," Draven answered, making it clear in those two words that there would be the promised consequences.

Marly swore, a crude word Grace hated to hear coming from her little girl's mouth. But before she could step forward to speak, Draven dealt with it neatly.

"That's another hour."

"That's not fair!"

"Life isn't."

The girl glared at him, then turned on her heel and stomped back the way she had come, toward a pile of native plants she'd obviously been assigned to sort. It was part of the price of building here, that the plan had to include returning the site to as natural a state as possible.

"You're being a little tough on her," Grace said as she came around the corner of the trailer.

Draven turned to look at her. "Yes," he agreed, surprising her. It took the wind right out of her sails.

"You don't think too tough?"

"She has options." He paused, then added, "You, too."

"What are my options?"

He gave her that half shrug she was coming to know. "She goes back."

"Back?" she asked, thinking he meant back home to the States. And then it hit her. "The police, you mean. That's no option."

"Better than the other."

"What other?"

"Give up. Let her keep on that path."

She winced. He nodded.

"It's long, twisted, evil and sometimes deadly."

Grace knew he was right, but it still stung. But the vision he painted with those stark words hurt so much more. She swallowed hard, sucked in some air and tried to keep her voice level.

"I've been trying for over a year to get through to her. Nothing I did worked. At least you have her attention."

He looked at her for a long, silent moment. Then he nodded. He started to turn away, apparently to go back to whatever he'd been doing when Marly had interrupted him to complain. And then he looked back at her, an odd expression on his face.

"She'll be all right," he said.

"Thank you," she said, wondering why he looked like saying it was painful.

Draven fingered the scar on his face as he stood in the dark, contemplating his sleeping quarters. He caught himself doing it, and yanked his hand away. Most of the time he forgot the scar was there, at least until somebody reminded him. Few people were tactless enough to do it in words, but their eyes gave them away. The widening in shock when they first looked at him was hard to miss.

He didn't know why he was aware of it now. But it had become more frequently lately, in his mind yet another sign that he was not the man he'd been.

I wish Josh would just let go, he thought.

But he knew better. Josh Redstone was careful about who he chose, but once you were in, he'd go to the wall for you.

Even if—especially if—you couldn't do it for yourself.

Which apparently he couldn't, he thought sourly, since he was standing here like an idiot pondering things that had no answers, something he normally didn't do much.

Which just proved yet again that, at least at this point, he wasn't normal.

Yanking his uncharacteristically unruly mind back to business, he contemplated his surroundings. And the standing orders from Josh; Redstone Security was not the police. *Thank goodness,* Draven thought; he knew a lot of cops, and nearly all of them felt handcuffed by the system they were trying to work within. So while they weren't limited in that way, Josh's policy was if they came across something criminal, they handed it over to the authorities.

Unless one of their own had been hurt. Then, for Josh, all bets were off.

But no one from Redstone had been hurt here. Yet, at

least. So Draven's job was to keep it that way, and secondarily to keep the job going. That obviously meant stopping the vandalism. Whether that process included finding out who was behind it and turning them in, or simply making it too risky for whomever it was to continue, was up to him.

Decision made, he went into the trailer to grab his bedroll, came back out and tossed it up on the roof of the trailer. He hoisted himself up after it, spread out the blankets, and stretched out on them. He left his boots on this time, thinking if something happened he'd have to jump in a hurry.

But he'd be able to hear better outside, and the spot gave him a better view all around. They didn't know when the Zodiac had been sunk, but the other strikes had come at night, so he would be on guard. At least this close to the equator he didn't have to wonder when sunrise was. The sunrise and sunset were nearly always somewhere between five-thirty and six-thirty.

He looked up at the tropical sky, felt the warm breeze on his skin and thought of the other places he'd spent nights like this. Places that were much more unpleasant, inherently much more dangerous.

His cell phone vibrated against his side, and he took it out. A glance at the screen told him it was Redstone headquarters. The timer also told him it was nearly midnight here, so nearly eleven back there. It seemed odd that there was only an hour difference in the time zones; this place seemed much farther away than that.

He flipped the phone open and answered.

"Draven."

"News?"

Ah. St. John. "Still only a few incidents. Minor, except for a Zodiac."

"I heard."

"News?" he asked in turn. Josh had once said listening to them talk was like listening to Morse code, only in English. He supposed that wasn't far wrong.

"Info checks out. The nickname's known in Belize, Guatemala, couple more. So far, research hasn't uncovered the real name."

The man known as *el mercader* was very careful, then, if the Redstone research team hadn't been able to dig that up. Very careful.

"They will. Eventually," Draven said. They always did. But he still wasn't convinced the man was their problem. It was just too predictable.

Things become predictable by happening frequently, he told himself, *so don't discount any possibilities.*

"Need anything?"

To not be here, Draven answered silently.

"Not for this," he said, and disconnected. If Josh had told St. John, or if, in that disconcerting way the man had, he simply knew about his resignation, then he'd understand the blunt answer. If not, then it didn't matter.

Something else Josh had said that morning when he'd tried to quit came back to him. He'd asked if Draven thought he would let his top man go without a fight.

"St. John might have something to say about that ranking," he'd said.

"St. John is nobody's man," Josh had replied. "If he walked out tomorrow I wouldn't be surprised. But you…"

And just like that, Josh had hit his most vulnerable point. He, and Redstone, had earned Draven's loyalty. And that was the real reason he'd let Josh revoke his leave.

Draven laid back down on the bedroll. He tried to think about the job at hand, but the end of that scene was jabbing at him. The stiff, formal way he'd said to Josh, "I can no longer do my job adequately."

Josh's mouth had twitched, and in the lazy drawl that fooled so many into thinking he was less brilliant than he was, he said, "I've got news for you, my friend. You've *never* done your job just 'adequately.'"

While the compliment, coming from this man, pleased him, it made it all the more impossible to explain why he had to quit.

He couldn't trust himself anymore.

He didn't sleep but dozed, waking regularly to look and listen. He'd always slept very lightly, and his years on the edge had only honed the habit to a fine edge, where the slightest thing out of the ordinary would bring him fully awake and alert. Occasionally there was the sound of some night creature moving, but his subconscious processed and categorized the sounds without truly waking him.

When it happened this time, it took him a moment to realize that it hadn't been a sound that had awakened him. He kept his eyes closed and listened, but heard nothing. He drew in a deep breath to hold it, so his own breathing wouldn't mask any slight sound. And it was then he got it; the faintest, merest tinge of a smell.

Propane.

He was up and moving in an instant. He dropped from the roof of the trailer to the ground and took off to the west in a low, swift run.

The only thing that used propane on the site was the power generator, and it was some distance away, tucked back behind some shrubbery to minimize the noise during the day while it ran to charge the batteries on all the self-contained housing units and motor homes, and power whatever else needed to be run. At night it automatically switched off in the interest of peaceful sleep for those staying on the site.

The propane smell got stronger as he got closer, until it was so strong he knew he was going to have to be careful.

The stuff could be lethal if you breathed in enough of it, but it would make you light-headed long before that. And he needed to be thinking clearly.

He was thankful for the breeze that had wafted the heavier-than-air gas up to him. He didn't want to think how ugly the explosion could be at the slightest spark. And if the leak hadn't been found before the timer tried to fire the engine in the morning, just the spark plug could do it.

He crouched down behind the bushes that masked the generator from the rest of the site. He listened, but still heard nothing. He slipped around the shrubbery and over to the big, metal housing-encased machine.

It took only a minute to find the problem. The line running to the generator from the five-hundred-gallon tank had been cut. With the valve still open, the gas was escaping at a steady rate.

In a moment he'd found the valve and turned it off to stop the flow. That done, he retreated, heading into the breeze for some clean air. Once he was sure he'd cleared out his lungs, he did a search of the surrounding area. He found some footprints, but had no way of knowing if they were from a suspect or one of their own. They were from bare feet, which might indicate a local, except that many of the crew took advantage of the mild weather to free their feet from heavy work boots or shoes when they were off shift for the day.

He also found a broken branch on one of the bushes. It looked fresh enough to have been done tonight. He continued in the direction suggested by the break, and found more of the bare footprints here and there until he reached the road. Whoever it was, they hadn't been in a hurry; the steps were evenly spaced and at a comfortable walking distance. Closer together than his own strides, so likely the suspect was shorter, but there was no sign he'd been running or even walking fast.

Likely he parked a vehicle and walked in. A quick, silent slice and he was done. Back in the vehicle and gone. And smart enough—or lucky enough—not to pull the car or truck off onto the shoulder and leave tire tracks in the soft ground. Combined with the bare feet instead of recognizable shoe prints, he was leaning toward smart.

Which took this whole thing into a different ballpark.

He searched the area thoroughly, but found nothing else he could connect to the incident. He made his way back to the propane tank. He found and shut off the timer switch so it wouldn't try to turn the generator on before they got the line repaired. Then he turned his thoughts to what to do next.

He could simply sit here and wait for the breeze to dissipate the remaining fumes.

And hope like hell nobody had the need for a midnight cigarette, he thought.

Or that nobody turned on an electrical switch anywhere near a buildup of the heavy gas. Or started a vehicle. Or any one of the numerous things that could spell disaster in the presence of propane vapor. With the moisture here in the tropical air static electricity thankfully wasn't likely, so simple movement shouldn't be a problem.

But if something did go, an explosion could follow the gas trail back to the source, and if that big tank went up it would leave a crater the size of a large asteroid hit, and they'd all probably be buried in it one way or another.

The other option was waking everybody up to warn them. Of course, if he did that, their first instinct would be to turn on a light. And while the chances were slim the buildup was heavy enough that far away for that to cause an explosion, he couldn't say there was no chance at all. He couldn't even go around and disconnect the battery power for each rig, for fear of causing an arc.

He could just check for any low pockets where the gas might have accumulated. But he wasn't sure how sensitive his nose was, if he would still be able to smell well enough after taking in so much of the vapor. But it was better than doing nothing, he thought.

He'd start with Grace's motor home. He told himself it was only logical that he start there because it was the closest.

By the time he got back to the site, he almost had himself convinced.

Chapter 7

Grace tried to slow her racing heart with deep breaths. She listened for a repeat of the sound that had awakened her. She heard nothing, but knew something had awakened her.

Marly again?

She reached for her crutch, got up and went to the doorway to peer into the other room. Her daughter was facedown on the foldaway bed, snoring softly, no doubt exhausted from the work she'd done today. It was a new experience for the girl, working that hard physically, and Grace couldn't help thinking it would do her good.

But that didn't tell her what she'd heard.

She crept past Marly and unlocked the front door of the motor home. She grabbed the flashlight she always kept handy, thinking the heavy, metal tube would serve as a weapon if necessary. It wasn't until she'd eased the door open that she remembered the inflatable, and realized a flashlight wouldn't be much defense against the kind of knife that had sunk it.

She was considering retreating and locking both her and Marly safely inside when she caught the faintest whiff of something on the air. She'd been on enough sites that used generated power to recognize it quickly.

Propane.

Fear spiked through her. She'd once seen a tanker carrying the fuel explode after a collision, and it was not a thing she ever wanted to see again. The resultant fire had literally burned through the asphalt roadway, and left the truck itself a melted pile of unrecognizable metal.

She had no choice now, she had to find out why she was smelling it all the way over here. She pulled the door open and went quickly down the two metal steps.

And nearly screamed when a huge, dark figure suddenly loomed up in front of her.

"What are you doing?"

Draven. It was Draven.

She repeated the knowledge to her once-again hammering heart, but it didn't seem to be listening. She had to gulp for air before she could answer.

"Testing my heart rate, apparently," she snapped, straining to keep her voice low to avoid waking Marly.

"Sorry."

She decided to drop it there; she supposed skulking around in the dark was part of his job, after all.

"I smelled propane," she said.

He nodded. "Line's been cut."

She let out a compressed, disgusted breath. She'd been hoping it was some sort of malfunction or normal kind of leak. "You shut the valve?"

"Yes."

"Another big knife?"

"More likely the same one."

"In the same hands?" She knew he couldn't be sure, since

no one had yet been seen, but she wanted his gut feeling. She suspected it was rather finely tuned by now.

"If I had to guess, yes," he said, confirming her own thoughts.

She turned her head and took a deep breath, then turned the other way and did the same.

"It'll be clear shortly," he said. "Stuff lingers."

"Are we safe now?"

"Not enough left to be a problem without direct ignition, I don't think."

She nodded. "I'll have Chuck Carlson fix it in the morning. He's good with that stuff."

He nodded in turn, then gave her a quick look up and down. "I'll watch till it's clear. Go back to bed."

For the first time, she realized she was standing here in front of him in just the old T-shirt and boxer shorts she slept in. And the shirt was worn thin, which made it comfortable but didn't hide much.

"Oh. Yes. I will," she said, feeling as if she had suddenly developed a stammer.

He nodded, and turned to go. Then he stopped and looked back at her.

"Next time, Grace, stay put and call me. It's my job, not yours."

She flushed, but hoped he couldn't see it in the darkness. "I'm not used to having to call someone." *Or someone to call,* she added to herself.

"Get used to it," he said.

And then he was gone. Grace went back inside, intending to head back to bed. But her legs felt suddenly weak, and instead she sank down onto the passenger's chair at the front of the motor home and felt herself tremble.

"It's the stress," she whispered. "That's all."

And it just happened to get worse when he was around. Because of what she associated with him. That's all.

After a few minutes, she checked once more on Marly, and went back to bed.

The heavy equipment was fine, Nick told him in the morning.

The propane line was fixed and the entire system had been checked, Chuck Carlson said.

The new inflatables had arrived right on schedule just before noon, and Draven had gone back underwater to attach and activate the motion alarm he'd asked for, which had come along with a few other things in the shipment with the boats.

The first thing he heard when he pulled himself out of the water was a young voice from behind him advising, "You're a mess."

He slicked the water out of his hair before he turned around to see Marly studying him—or rather his scars—intently.

"You're late," he said.

"You didn't tell me a time."

"I said morning."

"It is," Marly protested.

Draven glanced at his diver's watch. It was one minute to noon. "You skate the edge, don't you?"

She gave him a mutinous look. "What edge?"

"The edge," he said, his tone ominous, "of my temper."

"Oh." She apparently decided to cut her losses and dropped it. "What happened to you?" she asked with the bluntness of youth, indicating his scars.

"Which time?"

Her mouth quirked, as if she wanted to smile but wouldn't allow herself. "All of them."

"Knife, gun, shark and bomb."

Her eyes widened and her eyebrows shot up. "Shark?"

"Shark," he confirmed.

"Which one?"

"Guess."

She looked him up and down, her gaze halting on the semicircle of marks on his right calf. "Your leg, right?"

"Right."

"Wow."

"Didn't think so at the time."

Again the smile threatened, a little more of it getting through this time.

So, there's hope, he thought.

The momentary softening didn't last. A moment later she had her arms crossed in front of her, and was glaring at him.

"What do I have to do today, Mr. Boss?"

He studied her for a moment. He looked past the bluster in her tone, and the challenge in her posture. He saw what hovered beneath the façade, saw it and knew it for what it was, because he'd seen it so often.

He'd planned on more manual labor to drive the point home, but he suddenly changed his mind.

"Help," he said.

"Who?"

"Me."

She blinked. Then, suspiciously, "Help you what?"

"Set some traps."

It worked. She looked interested despite herself. "Traps?"

He nodded. "Surveillance cameras. Alarms. Trip wires. Snares."

With each word her eyes widened more. "Me? You want me to help with that kind of stuff?"

"Problem?"

"No! Beats sorting weeds, that's for sure."

The smile broke through completely then. And her enthusiasm grew when she realized he'd seriously meant for her to help, not just hold things for him. He used her to test the field of view for the cameras around the perimeter of the site. When she asked why no wires, he explained about the transmitters Ian had developed, and that all the images would be recorded back in the trailer.

"Taped?"

He shook his head. "Digital. New system." He gave her a sideways look. "Developed by the same guy who did your mother's foot."

The girl frowned. She was still angry with her mother, it seemed. He was very glad he didn't have to deal with that teenage moodiness. It was tough enough handling the little contact he was having.

Once the cameras were in place and turned on, he started out on the more primitive stuff.

"A trip wire? You mean like people trip over?"

"Yes. And they pull one end out of a box with an alarm."

"And that sets it off?"

He nodded. "And in this case, does a little extra."

"Extra?"

"Heard of a dye pack? In a bank robbery?"

"You mean the thing they put with the money that sprays the robber?"

"Exactly."

She looked at the little box they were setting up. "You mean these have those?"

"They do."

The smile became a grin. "Cool! What color?"

He blinked. Looked down at the alarm box.

"How are we gonna know what color to look for?" Marly asked with a touch of impatience.

"Good point," he muttered, and picked up the packet to read it. "Purple."

"Hey, my favorite color!"

"Congratulations. You can pass the word."

"Really? You mean to the crew?"

He nodded.

"Cool," she said again. He wondered what two "cools" in less than a minute were worth in teenage coin. "So what do I tell them? Watch for any purple people?"

He couldn't stop the corner of his mouth from twitching. "Pretty much."

"And report to you if they see any?"

He nodded. "No matter what their explanation is."

"Okay. What's next?"

"Lasers," he said.

She seemed to have given up trying not to grin. "Co—"

Draven held up a hand to cut her off. "Cool," he said.

"Yeah," she said, the grin getting even wider.

She helped him sight the laser beam projectors and the receivers, something he could have done by himself but it would have taken twice as long.

"So do they have those red beams like you see in the movies? And if you break the beam, it's set off?"

"No, and yes."

Her brow furrowed. "No red beams?" She sounded disappointed.

"Not visible. Defeats the purpose."

"I guess it would," she said, although she still sounded let down.

When they were done with the lasers, she stood back and looked at where they'd put them.

"A lot of people walk through here all the time. Aren't they going to go off all the time?"

"Only on at night, like the inner set of cameras. But, yes, I'll be jumping at false alarms a lot."

"Then why do it?"

"Only takes one real one."

"I guess," she said, but she looked doubtful, as if running to false alarms wasn't the idea she'd had of his job.

When they were done there, she helped him carry the camera monitors into the trailer.

"Why four?" she asked as they lined them up on a counter at the back of the trailer. "We put up sixteen cameras."

"Four zones," he said. "Perimeter, beach, two in the actual construction area."

"The ones that will be off at night? 'Cause everybody's always walking around?"

He nodded.

"Four cameras in each zone?" she asked.

He nodded again as he started to hook up the first monitor.

"Then…each screen is divided into four pictures? Or do they rotate?"

He stopped and looked at her. "Divided. Know why?"

She thought a moment. "So you can always see all the cameras?"

"Exactly."

He gave her a nod of approval. This time her smile wasn't one of amusement, it was one of pleasure.

She watched closely as he connected the first and second monitors. When he started on the third, she turned the fourth so she could see the back. She seemed to be poking at the wires, and then he realized she was trying to wire it. He opened his mouth to stop her, but then stopped himself. She'd done fine on the other stuff, she was obviously bright, so he let her continue.

She was still fiddling with it when he finished, but he said nothing. He saw her glancing at the others, as if to confirm she'd done hers the same way. Then she stepped back and looked at him, silently inviting him to look.

He didn't.

"Let's fire them up," he said.

She stared at him. "Aren't you even going to look?"

He met her gaze. "Do it right?"

"I think so."

"All right, then."

The girl's jaw literally dropped. He'd trained enough new agents over the years, and enough ranger candidates in the army, to recognize he'd found a key here.

And when they turned on the monitors and they all worked, Draven gripped her shoulder for a moment and said, "Good job."

She smiled up at him. He felt how thin her young shoulder was under his hand. So fragile. And for the first time in his life, he thought he understood a little bit about parents who would do anything to protect their child.

They had a morning of peace. No more incidents, the grading had actually started, and Draven had time to enjoy watching Grace in her element. He'd done all he could do for now, with the cameras and other gear now installed and working. He knew that, but he was still wound up. He wasn't sure why, but he knew better than to deny the feeling. He'd learned early on that when his gut started screaming, it was usually about something his head hadn't figured out yet.

So, figure it out, he ordered himself.

He walked down toward the water. Since they faced west here, he could see the sun on its downward arc, and the water was reflecting the golden light. It would get darker, more orange as it continued the plunge. He dropped down on the sand, drew up his knees and rested his crossed arms on them.

He stared at the incoming surf. It wasn't big here, the reef took care of that. But the rhythm was the same, the sound as soothing as everywhere on the water. But it wasn't soothing him. It was doing nothing to ease the edginess he was feeling.

He heard faint sounds behind him and glanced over his shoulder. With an inward sigh he saw something approaching guaranteed to only increase his tension.

Grace.

She was wearing a pair of loose, almost flowing pants and a short, sleeveless sweater, both in a shade of blue that nearly matched the distant stretches of the sea. The outfit seemed to suit the location; she looked cool and tropical at the same time.

She had an almost bemused expression on her face as she came to a halt beside him.

"Do you mind?" she asked, gesturing toward the empty sand beside him.

He did, but he couldn't say so. Besides, he knew she wouldn't voluntarily seek him out unless there was something she needed to say. So instead he nodded, and she sat beside him. Smoothly, he noticed. She went down on the knee of her intact leg first, then went the rest of the way. She'd obviously figured out ways to do most things smoothly.

The breeze caught a gleaming strand of her dark hair, and she reached up to push it out of her eyes.

"You cut it." Yet another lapse, he thought. He didn't usually voice such things, merely observed and filed away.

"The prosthesis takes time in the morning. Something had to go."

He just looked at her while he processed that unexpected bit of information. He wondered if she realized what that simple act said about her. That she was practical, yes, but also that she was adaptable, flexible, willing and able to make the best of a difficult situation.

He wondered if she'd realized how good that haircut would look before she'd seen it.

"Suits you."

"I like it," she said. "It's easier, cooler and my hair's healthier."

And it makes your nape the sexiest thing on the planet.

He jerked his head back toward the water, as his thoughts careened out of control again. He didn't want her to see the sudden rise of heat reflected in his eyes. He wasn't sure he could hide it; it had been so long since he'd had to try.

And another sign, he thought. He who had the poker face that was second only to St. John, had lost that as well. He wasn't getting better. He was getting worse. True, he wasn't really on the promised leave, but this wasn't exactly a high-stress case.

"If I'm bothering you," she began.

Oh, you are, he muttered to himself. "No," he said.

"You looked deep in thought."

"Was. I'm too edgy. Feel like I overlooked something."

"I doubt that."

He gave the half shrug. "Trying to figure out what they'll try next."

She seemed to ponder that. "What would you do?"

"What?"

"You're the best at this. What would you do if you were on the other side?"

He drew back slightly. In fact, he often did just that, but he hadn't expected her to come up with it.

She mimicked his one-shouldered shrug. "It just seemed logical that by now you'd know how they think."

"You're right."

For a few minutes they sat in silence. It should have been comfortable, in this beautiful setting, but he felt as tightly wound as if he were heading into a fight against stacked odds. He didn't know, wasn't sure he wanted to know, if it was the situation or her presence that was making him feel this way. But the way he kept glancing at her, his own thoughts about her incredibly sexy nape rolling around in his head, told him which was more likely.

"Thank you," she said.

Yanked out of that particular reverie, he reassured himself that he hadn't really said that about her sexy neck aloud, so she couldn't be talking about that. It wasn't something she'd thank him for, anyway. Hardly.

He started to speak, then stopped, wondering when he'd started to feel everything she said needed an answer from him. With most people he simply let them talk until they got to the point, then answered if necessary, but with Grace he felt oddly compelled to respond to it all.

He compromised by staying silent but lifting an eyebrow at her in query.

"Marly. She's changed, especially the past two or three days. She's excited, enthused, maybe not cheerful but at least not sullen. And she's talking, even to me."

"Amazing."

Her mouth quirked before she added. "She's almost human again."

"Scared."

She drew back slightly. "What?"

"She's scared."

Grace frowned. "Of what?"

"Losing you."

Her eyes widened. "Losing me?"

"Almost did," he pointed out. "And she already knows her father doesn't want her."

"But she didn't lose me. And that's one of the reasons I brought her with me to this job, so she'd know it's normally not really dangerous."

"What shouldn't happen doesn't register when what did happen is taking up all the room."

Her gaze turned inward, as if she were searching for truth in his words. Probably wondering where he got off espousing theories about her child. Or any child.

Finally she gave a slow, thoughtful nod. Still, it was another moment before she spoke again. "But if she's afraid of that, then why is she pushing me away?"

He gave her the half shrug. "Trying not to need you so much, for when she does lose you."

She stared at him until he did something he rarely did; he dodged her steady gaze by turning his face back to the sea.

"For a guy who says he knows nothing about kids, you're awfully wise."

"Some things are universal."

"Like trying to avoid pain?"

"I've seen people who could withstand the worst kind of physical pain run like hell from the other kind. They don't want to be on either side of it, so they make sure nobody gets close enough to hurt or be hurt."

There was a long moment of silence, long enough to make him tense. When she spoke, in a soft, gentle voice, he knew he'd been right to be wary.

"Are you one of them?"

He drew in a breath. Made himself look at her. Made himself hold that steady gaze.

"Yes."

She didn't look surprised, only as if something she'd suspected had been confirmed. He supposed his reputation in this area preceded him almost as much as his reputation with Redstone Security. No one, but no one, got really close to John Draven.

He wondered why he'd admitted that to her. Why he had told her something that he normally wouldn't even talk about at all, to anyone. When he realized it was by way of a warning, his gut knotted. He could only hope she would heed the warning and keep her distance.

Because the longer he spent with her, the less certain he was that he could.

And then she startled him by asking one more question, one no one else had ever asked. Ever dared to ask.

"Do you like it that way?"

He was saved from having to answer that one.

A bone-shivering yell came from the direction of the construction site.

So much for peace.

Chapter 8

It was easy to spot the scene of the incident once they were back on the site. Most of the crew was clustered around the area where the building supplies for the very small, single gate terminal that would eventually be built were kept. As they got closer, they saw that there was a man on the ground, with Nick and two others kneeling beside him, and several others leaning over him.

Grace started to run, and on the soft ground he saw the first real evidence of her injury. He doubted she would welcome an offer of help, so he smothered the instinct. Once she got on more solid ground her stride evened out and she picked up speed.

When they got there they found Chuck, the man who'd fixed the propane line, lying on the ground amid a pile of cinder blocks. A couple of the men were still dragging the blocks off of him, so Draven had to assume he'd been at least partially buried under them. But he was conscious, talking to Nick, and recognized Grace when she knelt beside him.

"I'm okay," he said, but his face was pale and he winced when he sat up.

"I'll take him into the clinic in town," Nick said. "The doc there's a Brit. He'll check him out."

"Just get him out from under all this," she ordered, the sharpness of her voice the only outward sign of the strain Draven knew she had to be under.

His glance flicked to her. This was eerily reminiscent of the earthquake, and her own trauma of being trapped under building debris. It had to be sending hideous images racing through her head. Yet she stayed right there, her hand on the injured man's arm, assuring him he would be all right and that everything would be taken care of.

He'd always known she had physical courage. She wouldn't have come back the way she had if she didn't. But what she was doing right now showed serious mental courage, and he marveled at her strength.

He couldn't help thinking of their talk on the beach, when he'd as much as admitted he himself was an emotional coward. He felt even more of one now, witnessing this. True, in his case it was mostly habit and knowing that his work didn't make for stability for anyone involved with him, but he couldn't deny that not getting burned was a side benefit.

Reminding himself it was time to get back to work, he also knelt beside Chuck.

"What happened?" he asked.

"I saw the stack of cinder blocks leaning," he said. "One near the bottom had gotten pushed way out of line. Stupid, I tried to push it back and the whole thing came down."

"See anyone else around?"

"No."

"Anyone leaving?"

"No. Ouch," he said as, the last of the blocks cleared now,

Draven began to check for broken bones by pressing his ribs. "We were done for the day. I was heading to sign out."

Draven nodded and continued his inspection. He'd lost track of how many times he'd done this over the years, checked for injuries. Too often, he thought.

"Nothing obviously broken," he said.

"Except maybe that hard head," Nick joked.

"Yeah, yeah," the injured man said in exaggeratedly insulted tones. But Draven guessed that if he hadn't still had his hard hat on, they might be looking at something a lot worse than scrapes and bruises.

Draven stood up and nodded at Nick. "He's all yours."

One of the others had run to get a truck. There was a brief dispute while Chuck convinced Nick that he didn't need to lie down in the back, he could sit up just fine, then Draven watched as the crew helped get the injured man into a vehicle for transport to the small clinic in town. When Redstone was established, they'd provide an ambulance for the clinic, but for now they were on their own. He didn't think the man's condition would require anything they couldn't provide, or he would have called Redstone for an airlift.

Grace closed the door of the truck, reached in and patted Chuck's arm and told Nick to call as soon as they knew anything. Draven guessed she was not accompanying her crewman only because Nick was already going. She felt the same loyalty to them that they felt for her.

When the vehicle had pulled out and the crew began to return to what they'd been doing, Draven and Grace headed for the trailer. Grace needed to make a report to Redstone headquarters, and he wanted to check the video monitors.

"Do you think this was more of the same?" she asked.

"I don't know. This one was daytime. Not an obvious booby trap."

"Obvious?"

He nodded. "Whoever it is, wants us to know. So we'll know more is coming if we don't stop."

She stopped walking and turned to face him. "You mean they don't want to slow the project down, they want to shut it down?"

"That's my guess."

She let out a sigh. "So much for my clever idea."

"Idea?"

"I had myself half convinced this drug king or whoever it was just wanted time to move and after that things would calm down."

She gave him a sideways look, as if expecting him to call her a fool.

"Not a bad theory," he said. "But no sign of *el mercader* packing up the china."

"You've checked?"

He nodded. "Lot of money sunk into that compound of his. And he's worked at keeping his nose clean here."

"So he won't give it up easily."

"No. If it is him."

"You don't think it is?"

"Not convinced yet," he said, leaving it at that. They began to walk again.

"So, do you think this was an accident?"

"Could it have been?" he asked in turn.

She considered that, then reluctantly said, "Yes, it could have. We don't usually have accidents like that, but I can't say it doesn't ever happen."

"Reserve judgment on this, then."

She nodded as they reached the trailer and went up the stairs. To his surprise Marly was there, and when they stepped inside she whirled on them.

"Where have you been?" she yelped. "I've been waiting and waiting so I could tell you."

"Don't be rude," Grace began, but stopped when Draven held up his hand.

"Tell what?" he asked the girl.

After a triumphant glance at her mother, she looked at Draven and said, "I found something!"

"Found?"

She nodded excitedly. "I've been looking at the recordings, from the cameras."

"What did you see?"

"I'll show you!"

Eagerly she picked up a DVD case from the table that held the monitors. She seemed nearly giddy as she ran over to her mother's desk, sat and pushed the disc into the drive on the computer. The software started up automatically, and quickly a small image appeared on the screen. For a moment it was simply the camera view of the area where the accident had happened.

"This was the day we put the cameras in," she said. Then the picture flickered and steadied again.

"The block," Grace said.

Draven nodded. In the clip, the huge load of cinder blocks was clearly visible. As was the block Chuck had talked about, far out of line with the rest. Looking at it, it was easy to see how the entire thing had toppled.

"So you see, it was already crooked by the time we turned the recorders on. And I figure most of the guys would notice that, just like Mr. Carlson did, so he must have been the first to see it, so it couldn't have been that way long, maybe just since the night before."

She finally stopped, probably because she had to take a breath, Draven thought. When Marly realized both adults were staring at her, she didn't start up again. She stared back, waiting, her body wiredrawn with excitement.

"The propane," Grace whispered.

Draven nodded. "Same night."

"It could have been a diversion rather than an attack?"

"Both," Draven said.

"We'd better look around for anything else like that stack of blocks, then," Grace said. Then, to her daughter she continued, "That was great, honey. And you were clever, to figure that out."

The girl only shrugged.

Draven nodded in agreement with Grace's assessment. "Good job," he said.

At his words, the girl beamed. Grace shot him a sideways glance. The difference in reactions couldn't have been more blatant. He felt like telling the girl she was being beyond stupid, if she cared more about the opinion of some man she'd known all of a few days over her mother's. Especially when that man was him. And that mother was Grace.

He didn't dare look at Grace. He had a feeling this was the teenager trying to manipulate them, or at the least manipulate her mother, and he didn't want to play into her hands.

"Now you can get an early start on sorting the last of those plants in the morning."

She looked so crestfallen he wondered how any parent ever hung on to discipline.

"Oh, to be doing a nice, plain, gravel runway," Grace said rather glumly.

"You always say that," Nick said with a chuckle.

She smiled. He was right. And she also knew it was a sign of how much she'd relaxed that she'd slipped into the old habit.

And it was all thanks to Draven. The string of uneventful days had stretched into a week now, because of all he'd done. Chuck was back at work with a clean bill of health, no more accidents or sabotage incidents.

And a lot had been accomplished. Clearing, grading, leveling, it was all done. They were nearly at the point of putting down the first layer, the cement-treated base. Then would come the reinforced concrete layer, and finally a layer of extra-strength concrete made that way by a new additive the Redstone lab had come up with.

If it lived up to the advance billing, the runway should last twice as long as previous structures, with minimal cracking and half the maintenance, before it had to be resurfaced. And if it did that, the commercial applications for airports and roads were tremendous. They could save the public millions of dollars over the long term.

"Are you going into town for the mail?"

Grace turned to look at her daughter. Despite her changing attitude toward Draven, she still hadn't let go of her resentment toward her mother, as evidenced by the abruptness and impatient note in the question. And her body language; the crossed arms and the angle of the chin practically shouted that she hated even talking to her.

With an effort Grace kept her voice even. "I may. Later."

"Can't I just get a yes or no?"

At the waspish tone of her voice, Nick cleared his throat and muttered something about a delivery and excused himself. He didn't quite run, but Grace guessed it was a close thing.

"Congratulations, Miss Congeniality," Grace said. She'd tried, but she was tired of being singled out for her own child's scorn.

"Hey, it was just a question. I can't help it if he didn't like it."

Grace reined in her temper and bit back the retort that was on the edge of her tongue. "Aren't you supposed to be working?"

"I don't care. I've had it. The other day was fun, with the cameras and stuff, but now he wants me moving rocks."

So, her rapport with Draven was conditional. As long as she liked what was happening, she liked him.

"If you quit, you're going to have a hard time finishing paying back Mr. Ayuso."

She shrugged. "You can pay him. You were about to anyway, before *he* stopped you."

Grace went very still at the way she said it. "That was a fast turnaround. Just days ago Mr. Draven was your pal."

Marly snickered. "Is that what you call him?"

"No. It's what you should call him."

The shrug again. She was getting mightily tired of them, both this one and Draven's one-shoulder version.

"Whatever," the girl said. "He doesn't really like me. He doesn't like kids at all."

"He isn't comfortable," she corrected, "because he hasn't been around them."

"Right." The girl waved her hand, in a gesture indicating how little she cared. "So, when you get the mail, you can pay the shop guy."

Grace took a deep breath. Despite the fact that the change apparently hadn't lasted, there had been a change, which was more than she'd been able to accomplish on her own.

"No," she said. "No, I can't."

"What?"

"You heard me. You keep saying you're not a child anymore. Handling your own responsibilities is part of that."

"Fine!" Marly snapped. "Just fine. I should have known I couldn't count on you."

"To love you, protect you and be a parent, you can always count on me. To help you get off easy when you mess up, or be your buddy instead of your mother, no. I've tried that. And I don't like how it came out."

The girl muttered something under her breath, something Grace couldn't make out. She let it pass, deciding one battle at a time was all she could handle. But when her daughter turned on her heel and marched off in an obvious snit, she felt a wave of near exhaustion overtake her. Nothing wore her out like conflict with the child she loved so much, but sometimes wanted to send away until she turned eighteen.

Maybe she would go in and get the mail, she thought. It wasn't her job, but she enjoyed it so did it anyway. It had only been a couple of days since she'd been in to the small post office window in the back of the general store, but there likely were some things for the crew. Nick in particular had a loving wife who constantly sent him whatever she thought would feel like a bit of home to him.

She decided to go, hoping the drive might clear her head. She checked to see if anyone needed anything. Everyone except Draven, that is; she felt better if she simply avoided him altogether. It had been difficult to approach him on the beach. And not just because every time she saw him all those awful memories flooded back. It was also because this was a setting for love, for romance, and the very idea made her uncomfortable.

She took one of the pickup trucks that wasn't needed at the moment. When she started it, the radio came on to a Caribbean station out of Belize City. The music was upbeat and she left it on, thinking it might help lift her spirits. By the time she pulled out onto the main road, she was already feeling better.

Chapter 9

"Seen Grace?"

The man on the grader shook his head. "Not in the last hour or so."

Draven felt an odd sort of pressure building inside him. This was the third person he'd asked who hadn't seen Grace for too long for his comfort. He'd checked the trailer, and her motor home, and everywhere work was going on, all the places she would usually be. Nothing. It was out of character for her, and any change in routine right now made him edgy.

Not that she had to check in with him anytime she went somewhere. She'd left the site before, for this errand or that, and he hadn't known. But she'd not been gone this long before.

Nor, he thought suddenly, had it bothered him. Not like this, anyway. But right now her simply being out of sight was bothering him. And he wasn't sure why.

So, figure it out, he told himself. And his own thought reminded him of what else he needed to figure out, what Grace had said to him on the beach.

He set off to check the perimeter, as he did often during the day. He did his best thinking off by himself, and right now he had the feeling his best thinking was what he needed.

"I've told Sergeant Espinoza he must go after *el mercader,* but he has not done anything. I begin to wonder why," Mayor Remington said, wringing his hands.

"I'm sure you have," Grace said.

"I cannot tell you how upset I am, that this man is on my island to begin with, let alone that he is interfering with your work."

Interfering wasn't the word she'd use, not after that too-near miss with Chuck, but she didn't say so. It also wasn't "his" island; Redstone owned from the border of the airstrip site south. But again she said nothing. The man was obviously upset, and she didn't want to make it worse.

He had flagged her down as she was walking through the grocery store to the post office window at the back. He looked as if he'd been wadding up what hair he had, and his shirt was damp with sweat. Of course, why he would wear a rayon shirt in this climate was beyond her.

But she knew he was genuinely concerned, so when he asked she told him, yes, they'd had more incidents since he'd last heard, but nothing recent. Redstone Security, she told him, had taken care of that.

"You're certain? *El mercader* is very clever."

"Redstone Security is the best," she told him. *And Draven is the one who made it that way.* "I'm not worried any longer, so don't you worry."

She felt a little ridiculous, reassuring the mayor, but it was true. She felt the project was much safer now. Draven had seen to that.

"Good," he said. "This airstrip will be a good thing for my island."

"Redstone will be good for your island," she promised.

She managed to break free of him then, and continued back to pick up the mail. The clerk, a friendly woman named Yvette, greeted her cheerfully, and said, yes, they had some mail waiting. While the woman gathered it up Grace asked about her granddaughter, always guaranteed to bring on an excited stream of chatter and a display of the latest photographs. She responded enthusiastically, exclaimed appropriately, which wasn't difficult; the child was a little beauty with huge, dark eyes.

Coming had been a good idea, Grace decided as she walked back to the truck with the armful of mail. She felt much better now, just getting away for a while. Although she was a little concerned about Sergeant Espinoza after what the mayor had said. She'd have to mention it to Draven.

She got into the truck and set the mail beside her. She started the engine and quickly rolled down the windows to let the heat that had built escape. After she fastened her seat belt, she checked the box addressed to Nick before starting out, to make sure it was secure on the seat.

She smiled, wondering what his wife had sent this time. There were always magazines from home, which Nick handed off to his eager co-workers, usually some home baked cookies—he wasn't quite so generous with those—and a selection of miscellaneous things that often had more than one crew member sighing for home.

Funny, people came to this tropical place from far away, thought of it as paradise and were reluctant to leave. But her crew was homesick. It was different being here for work, she supposed. And being away from family always took a toll. She'd seen more than one marriage crumble under the strain of constant travel. Including her own.

Of course, that had been only one of the problems she and Russell had had. He hadn't liked her choice of careers, either. Although he never actually said it, she suspected he'd wished she was in a more traditionally feminine field. And he had continually sniped at Redstone, in the manner of a person trying to raise himself up by tearing down better people.

But the most critical problem had always been the simple fact that he no longer wanted to be a father. Or Marly's father, she amended, not that it made any difference. His indifference to the girl who tried so hard to win his approval, who was still trying even in the face of his total rejection, hurt Grace more than anything Russell could ever do to Grace herself.

She smothered a sigh; this was old, worn ground and there was no point in going over it again. With an odd little start she realized that this could be credited to Draven as well; since the sabotage had started she'd been too distracted by that to spare even a thought for her ex. Until now.

She pondered this as she drove back to the site. So much had changed since Draven had come here. Just like it had the first time he'd come into her life.

Sometimes she wondered just how accurately she remembered that day. She'd spent so much time trying not to, but some images seemed inescapable. And one of them was Draven's face when he'd told her what he was going to do. She hadn't realized until much later how unusual that was, for him to show any emotion at all.

He certainly didn't now, she thought. She could never be sure what he was really thinking. Not that it mattered, of course, but—

The truck backfired. The loud crack made her jump. That must have made her jerk the wheel, because the truck suddenly careened sideways.

No, not a backfire. A blowout. A tire.

She barely had time to realize it before, with a sickening

lurch, the truck began to roll. The slope wasn't steep, but it was enough. Her seat belt dug into her as the passenger side hit the ground. Side. Top. Other side.

And in that moment she remembered the lagoon at the bottom of the slope.

There was no sign of any disturbance along the perimeter, but Draven kept walking.

What would you do if you were on the other side? Grace had asked.

What would he do? If, say, this airstrip was being built by the drug lord, and his assignment was to stop it by whatever means necessary? And so far, attacks on the project hadn't worked? What would he do?

He stopped dead in his tracks. His stomach plummeted. He should have realized this long ago. It was the final vicious piece of evidence that proved he was past it, that he shouldn't be here at all. There was no excuse for this not occurring to him until now.

He knew exactly what he'd do next if he was that guy on the other side. He'd go after the one person whose removal would bring everything to a halt.

He'd go after Grace.

He headed back to the work site at a run, leaping shrubbery and fallen trees. The trailer was still empty, and there was no sign she'd been back here. He started looking for Nick. If anybody on the crew knew where she was, he should. Unfortunately he was also sometimes hard to find. Being a typical Redstone employee, he ran every piece of machinery there was, wherever and whenever it was needed and the regular operator wasn't available.

He was heading for the compactor he'd last seen Nick running when he caught a glimpse of Marly sitting beside the native plants she was supposed to have finished sorting so the replanting could start. He changed directions abruptly and headed that way.

"Where's your mother?" he asked when she looked up as he got within a few feet.

"I. D. K. and I. D. C."

Her tone was immediately recognizable as sarcastic, but it took him a split second to translate the verbal shorthand into "I don't know and I don't care." Exasperation at her shot through him.

"No time for your moods. Where is she?"

She looked startled by his words, or the fierceness of them. "How should I know? She's the one who keeps me on a leash, not the other way around."

Draven knelt down to get on her level, well knowing the effect his stare had on people when he wanted it to. And he wanted it to now.

"When you're being a bitch, you should be on a leash."

The girl's eyes widened and she drew back. And then she met his gaze and paled. She wasn't too young to see it, he thought, that thing in his eyes that made people far more dangerous than this girl quail. He supposed he shouldn't use it on a child, but this was too important. He'd use whatever he had to use.

He asked again, in a deadly quiet voice. "Where is she?"

"She...might have gone to get the mail. In town."

He stood, and turned to go without a word. Then he looked back, not sure why he felt the need to try again to get through to this child.

"While you're sitting there, maybe you should think hard about what your life would really be like without her."

He caught up with Nick. The man confirmed what Marly had said, that the last thing he'd heard under discussion was a trip to town for the mail.

"But that was well over an hour ago. If she went, she

should have been back by now." Unlike Marly, Nick was quick to pick up on Draven's growing tension. "What's wrong?" he demanded.

"Just my gut," Draven said.

"You think she's in trouble?"

Draven hesitated. He wasn't one for involving civilians in his work. But if Grace had been gone for an hour on an errand that should have taken fifteen minutes, there was only one answer to Nick's question. And it might take more than one person to logistically handle.

"Possible," he said.

Before he could say any more Nick was off the machine and pulling off his work gloves.

"Let's go," he said, and headed toward the area where the auxiliary vehicles were parked.

When they were in the last pickup truck, before he started the engine, Nick looked at Draven.

"You got some kind of weapon?"

"Yes."

Nick studied him for a moment, and Draven wondered if he'd deduced that was why he was driving, so that Draven could keep his hands free.

Nick left it at that, to Draven's relief, and they started to move.

If the cay had traffic cops they would surely have been after Nick on this run. Draven was glad; it saved him from having to ask the man to step on it.

"We see Yvette first?" Nick asked at the edge of town.

"Post office?"

"Such as it is," he answered.

"Look for the truck first, then there."

Nick nodded. They drove the main street, checked the few side streets, with no luck. Nick glanced at Draven, who nodded to indicate the post office was next.

Draven followed as Nick led the way through the small store that seemed to carry everything from produce to hammers. The woman behind the counter in the back smiled as they reached the window, and said hello to Nick.

"Hi, Yvette," the man said. "You seen Ms. O'Conner?"

"Grace? She was just here this afternoon."

"When?" Draven asked, only aware of the tension in his voice when he saw the woman frown.

"Just after lunch. Maybe…one?"

Damn, Draven thought. *Definitely over an hour ago.*

"Did she say where she was going?" Nick asked the woman.

"No. I thought she was going right back." She smiled at him. "She had picked up your package, and said she knew you'd be anxious to get it."

Nick at least remembered to thank the woman; Draven was already halfway to the door.

The size of Matola City was an advantage in this case; Draven took one side of the main street and instructed Nick to take the other. Within half an hour they'd hit every open business and service, only to come up empty. No one else seemed to have seen Grace.

"Now what?" Nick asked.

Draven felt a qualm as the man looked at him for the solution. He was used to this. It was who he was. Redstone people looked to him for answers to things like this. When the darker side of real life intruded into their world, it was John Draven they turned to for help. But in this instant, at this moment, he didn't know what to do.

Never in his adult life had he felt like this. In the service, or with Redstone. No matter what the situation, he'd always been able to *do*. Something.

It's finally happened, he thought. He'd shut down completely. Just as he'd feared. Just as he'd expected.

He'd just never expected it to be at a time when he desperately didn't want it to happen. That's what he'd been trying to avoid by quitting.

"What should we do?" Nick asked.

Draven's stomach clenched, the only response from a gut that was usually utterly reliable in coming up with strategy. Something. Anything.

If your gut's silent, use your head, he ordered himself. Draw on experience. He had enough of that. What would he normally do in this situation?

"Backtrack," he said. "Trace her route."

Nick nodded as if Draven had come up with the best possible plan. He trailed after Nick as he headed back to their vehicle, feeling as if he were doing it because he couldn't think of anything else to do.

Draven sat in the passenger seat, thinking he'd never felt so much like exactly that, a passenger. He was no longer the man in charge, no longer the go-to guy. He'd known it was coming. And perhaps he should have known that when it hit, it would be at the worst possible time. He should have—

"I think I see something."

He looked up as the truck slowed down.

"Over there," Nick said, pointing.

Draven looked. He saw what the man meant, the disturbance in the dirt at the edge of the road.

"Stop," he said.

Before the truck had stopped rolling he was out and heading for the place Nick had spotted.

Tire tracks. There were tire tracks on the shoulder. Tracks that showed every evidence of a skid. And just over the lip of the road he could see the tops of shrubs that had been bent, twisted, smashed.

His breath jammed in his throat. He had to force himself to take that last step to look down the slope. Force himself, because he knew what he was going to see at the bottom of the slope. And when he got there, he saw it.

The truck Grace had been driving.

Upside down.

Cab under water.

Draven heard a shout just before he hit the water. He ignored it. He was focused only on that upended truck, as he had been throughout his mad, crashing race down the slope. It didn't matter that logic told him it had happened too long ago. It didn't matter that logic told him if she was inside, she was dead. After all, she'd been written off before and had survived.

He was at the truck in seconds; the water wasn't deep, but it was deep enough to drown in. It was also murky. Unlike the water of the sea, the lagoon water was stationary enough for various plant organisms to flourish. He got to the cab. It had dug into the silty bottom a few inches. On some level his mind was registering that the silt had had time to settle, but he refused to let the significance of that in.

He grabbed the sill of the window and pulled himself down, trying not to stir up the bottom and cloud the waters. He knew the moment he got even with the portion left exposed that he'd never be able to get inside. He couldn't even be sure Grace could have gotten out.

He didn't want to look but knew he had to. He had to.

The cab was empty.

"Now you just hold on there," Nick said, grabbing Grace's arm and pulling her back from the water's edge. "That boy can hold his breath a mighty long time."

"But—"

"No sense in you going back in there, not when you're lucky to have gotten out."

"It's not that deep," she said. "If the truck hadn't rolled upside down, I would barely have gotten wet."

"Then you don't need to worry about him, do you?" Nick said, nodding toward the water.

Grace opened her mouth, stopped and frowned at him. "That was sneaky."

Nick grinned. "Yes, wasn't it? I— Ah, there he is."

Her head snapped around just in time to see Draven's head pop up, and hear him take in a gulp of air. The kind he hadn't needed diving to the sunken inflatable the other day. He hadn't been down that much longer, but obviously he'd used more of the air he'd stored in his lungs.

He got to where he could stand up in waist-deep water, lifting his arms to slick his dripping hair back and clear the salty water from his eyes. Grace stared at him, thinking all those wet T-shirt contests over the years had been held for the wrong gender. Her fingers curled into her palms.

And then he saw her.

He went very still. As usual his expression betrayed nothing, but she saw his chest rise sharply, then heard, even from where she stood, the long, soft exhalation.

"I shouted," she said, feeling a bit guilty that he'd plunged right past her and she hadn't realized what was happening until it was too late and he was already under. She supposed her reactions were still dulled from the shock.

He walked up out of the water and stopped before her. He seemed to hesitate, then reached out and gripped her shoulders. The heat of his hands made her feel suddenly chilled wherever he wasn't touching her.

"You're all right?"

She nodded. "I got out right away. I had the windows open, so all I had to do was find up."

He closed his eyes for a moment.

"It's not deep," she continued. "I could see sunlight."

He muttered something under his breath that she couldn't catch. He opened his eyes and slowly, as if it were a tremendous effort, released her. She tried not to protest the loss.

"Lucky," he said.

"Yes," she agreed. She glanced at Nick. "I was more upset about your package than anything."

"Good grief, girl," Nick said. "That doesn't matter. You're safe, that's what counts. What happened anyway?"

"A tire blew," she said.

Nick frowned. "A tire? Everything's got new rubber on it. I'm really careful in hot climates, you know that."

"Yes, I know. But I heard the pop when it went, and then the truck just careened sideways. I tried, but the shoulder wasn't wide enough for me to get it straightened out."

"Well, damn," Nick said. "When we get back, I'll check all the tires on the auxiliary vehicles, to make sure—"

"Don't bother."

They both turned to look at Draven.

"What?" Nick asked.

"The other tires are fine. The one that caused the crash was fine."

"But it blew," Grace explained again, wondering if perhaps he'd not heard her right, water in his ears or something. "I heard it."

"What you heard," he said grimly, "was a shot."

Chapter 10

"But I can't—"

"You can and will."

Draven spoke in that same grim tone he'd used when telling her the tire hadn't simply blown, when he'd realized someone had tried to hurt or even kill her. It reflected exactly how he felt, how he'd felt since the moment when he'd seen the truck upside down in the water.

She'd taken a shower to rinse off the residue from the lagoon. He'd liked that she hadn't worried about anything else, but had simply come out of the motor home's bathroom in a pair of cutoff jeans and a bright blue T-shirt, with her hair wet and slicked back, her face scrubbed clean... and sans the prosthetic. Clearly she wasn't bothered by him seeing her without it, but then, considering, why should she be?

They'd done a nice job cleaning up his mess, he thought. The end of her leg was tidy, and looked healthy. Even the scars weren't that noticeable now, merely pink instead of the angry red he'd last seen.

She was using a crutch, resulting in a hop-and-swing-type motion that was in stark contrast to the ease with which she used the artificial foot. He wondered if the prosthesis had been damaged. If it had been, they'd deal with it later. Redstone would ship out a new one if necessary.

"I can't just stay off the project!" she protested now.

"You'd rather stay off it by dying?"

She paled slightly, but her chin came up in stubborn determination. "We have a schedule to keep."

"You won't."

"What?"

"If you're not safe, there is no project."

Her brow furrowed. "What are you saying?"

"Safety of Redstone personnel is job one."

He wasn't exaggerating. Josh put nothing above the safety of his people. When the Redstone Bay resort project had been taken over by terrorists from a neighboring island, the entire security team had been sent in. When a Redstone bookkeeper's child had been kidnapped, it was Redstone Security who had effected the rescue. And he had personally gone after Redstone's own Harlan McClaren, the famous treasure hunter who had been the first to believe in and financially back Josh, when one of his famous expeditions had gone sour in Nicaragua.

Shutting a project down until it was safe again—or forever, if necessary—was hardly out of the realm of possibility for Josh.

"You stay off-site unless there's something both urgent and that can't be delegated or handled on the phone."

"According to who?" she asked, her tone suspicious.

"Me," he said bluntly. "Next. You go nowhere without me."

"Nowhere?"

"Nowhere."

"Please, sir," she said in a voice dripping with sarcasm, "may I go to the bathroom by myself, like a big girl?"

"Depends."

"On what? You?"

She was building up a good mad; he could feel it. It wasn't surprising, given her narrow escape. She'd proven before that when she was knocked down, she came up fighting. He'd once thought of her as a quiet sort, maybe even shy. But he realized now that his impression was wrong, that her quietness had to have been because she had focused all her energy and considerable drive on getting well fast. Because this woman was no shrinking violet, in any way. She was standing up to him now in a way few ever did.

He tried to keep his voice level but, uncharacteristically, some tension crept through as he ticked items off.

"I'm going to move your motor home."

"Why?"

"Higher ground. And more isolated."

"Isn't there safety in numbers?"

"Don't argue with me, Grace."

"I'm not arguing," she protested. "I'm asking a simple question."

He reined in his temper, something else he'd never had to worry about before.

"I want it situated so that I know anybody coming toward it is looking for you, not just wandering or lost or looking for someone else."

"And if they are?"

"I'll handle it."

"How?"

"My problem."

"No, it's—"

He cut her off, and continued to count off his instructions.

"You go nowhere without me. You go nowhere I haven't checked first. If I don't like it, anything about it, you don't go or I go in with you. I stay till you're done."

"Does that include my bedroom?" she asked sweetly.

Heat blasted through him, so fast and fierce he nearly wobbled on his feet.

"Don't tempt me," he muttered under his breath. And then, as his body clenched, he added silently, *Please, don't.*

She looked at him, the faintest spots of color flaring on her cheeks, and he realized she'd heard him. She looked at him, her eyes wide. She looked at him as if she didn't hate the idea of tempting him. As if it didn't repulse her.

He told himself it was shock, shock from her crash, shock that he would say such a thing. But the only one who seemed shocked was he himself; he never—ever—did things like this, not with a protectee. Which is what she had suddenly become.

He didn't know how to deal with this. It never happened to him. He felt many things for the people he protected or helped for Redstone; he even liked many of them.

But he'd never felt anything like this.

"Look," he said, his unaccustomed emotions making him resort to slow, complete sentences. "I wish it wasn't me. You'd be better off with somebody else, especially since I'm running at about half speed. But I'm what you've got."

Her brows furrowed again. "What's wrong?"

God, he couldn't believe how he was rattling on. *Cut to the chase,* he ordered himself.

"You've got to cooperate, Grace, because right now I'm all that's between whoever wants to shut this down and you. And Marly."

She gasped, and he knew she hadn't thought that far ahead, hadn't realized that if she was in danger, it was possible her daughter was, too. He knew he had to take advantage of that. He had to use any tool that would work.

"Whoever it is tried to kill or at least badly hurt you," he said softly.

"Maybe not me, specifically, maybe…"

Her voice trailed off as he looked steadily at her. It was natural to deny the possibility that someone actually had tried to murder you, but he didn't have time to work her through to acceptance right now.

"You, specifically," he said. "And if they're willing to do that, why would they stop short of using your daughter as leverage?"

"Who's going to use me as leverage?"

They both jerked around as Marly stepped into the motor home. The girl looked at Draven, and as if he'd asked, said, "I finished, okay? I came in to clean up."

He nodded, not knowing what else to do. Using Marly to scare Grace into cooperating was one thing, scaring the child was something else.

"What kind of leverage? What are you talking about?" Marly persisted. And then, belatedly, she seemed to realize her mother's state. "Why are you all wet? And your foot, you never take it off in the middle of the day."

Grace shot Draven a warning look he couldn't misinterpret. "I took a little dip, so I rinsed off the salt."

The girl frowned. "You don't do that, either. You never take off work to play."

Only then did she seem to notice Draven, too, was soaking wet. He hadn't taken the time to hit the shower in the hut set up for the crew; he'd been too focused on getting Grace to cooperate.

"And you," Marly said, "don't know *how* to play."

At that succinct assessment of them both, the girl muttered something that sounded like "Whatever," and turned her back on them both to walk toward the bathroom. Apparently forgetting about the leverage question. Judging from Grace's look of relief, that was a good thing. Right now, he'd take anything that made her happy, as long as it also made her cooperate.

"I'm going to be your shadow, Grace. You're going to have to live with it. It's the only way to keep you and your daughter safe."

There was a whoosh of air as the door of the bathroom was yanked open. "Safe?" Marly's voice was sharper, and they clearly weren't going to get off so easily this time.

Someone had told him once about the selective hearing of teenagers, that they heard only what you didn't want them to hear, but he'd never seen it in action before. He should have waited until the bathroom door was shut tight.

Feeling guilty that his lack of knowledge about kids had caused this, he tried to fix it, to go along with Grace's obvious desire to keep today's incident from her daughter.

"A precaution," he said.

Marly looked from her mother to him, then back to her mother again.

"You really think I'm stupid, don't you?"

Her voice was soft, not angry as it usually was. There was an undertone even Draven recognized as a young girl's pain, and would have even if he hadn't noticed the sudden glistening of the girl's eyes as tears brimmed.

Grace's eyes, he thought, and wondered what it must be like to look at another human being and see parts of yourself. He'd never thought about it before, but when he did now, all he could picture was a dark-haired boy with those same eyes. And that rattled him enough to keep him silent. Grace needed to deal with this anyway. And would do a much better job of it than he would.

"No, Marly, I don't think you're stupid at all," Grace finally said. "I know you're not. But I'm your mother. I'm supposed to protect you."

The girl stepped back into the room, her gaze now fastened on her mother's face.

"So there is something to protect me from," she said. She flicked a glance at Draven, but only for an instant. "And it has to do with you both being wet, doesn't it."

It wasn't a question. No, Marilyn O'Conner was hardly stupid. Draven waited. It was up to Grace now to decide what and how much to tell the girl.

"There's a chance," Grace began, "that these little incidents on the project aren't accidental."

"No kidding," Marly said sourly. "You think I didn't notice everybody being so jumpy? What's that got to do with you being all wet, and him, too?"

Something about her reaction and tone made Draven take the girl off his mental suspect list. Unless she'd gotten tangled up with somebody in the short time they'd been here, he didn't think she was connected.

Grace sighed. "I didn't get wet intentionally. The truck and I...ended up in the lagoon outside of town."

Marly blinked. "How did—" She stopped. Draven saw her figure it out, saw her face pale. "Somebody ran you off the road?"

Grace took in a deep breath. Draven could see she didn't want to tell her about the shot, but didn't know how else to explain.

"In a manner of speaking," Draven said. "She wasn't hurt, but we're going to be very careful from now on."

Marly looked at him. "Why are you talking funny?"

It was Draven's turn to blink.

"What?" He definitely wasn't used to the twists and turns of the teenage mind.

"You never talk like that. Like a regular person."

"Thanks," he said, his mouth twisting wryly.

Marly shrugged and let it go. "What do you mean, careful, and who's we?"

"Those present," Draven said.

"And?" Marly prompted for the answer to the first part of her question.

Draven glanced at Grace and waited. After a long moment, during which Marly looked from one to the other as if their silent stares were a tennis match, Grace finally let out an exasperated-sounding breath of resignation.

"Go ahead," she said. "Tell her."

Great, he thought, imagining the teenager's reaction to being told she was to be more restricted than before. And he wasn't stupid, either, he knew perfectly well this was Grace's way of letting her own aversion to this whole thing be known.

Get it over with, he told himself. And rattled off the same list of limitations and orders he'd given Grace.

The girl's eyes widened with every statement. And when he was done, to his surprise, all she said was a very quiet, almost meek, "Oh."

"Any questions?" he asked, still a bit startled at her non-reaction.

She shook her head.

"Comments?"

She met his gaze, with more steadiness than some grown men he'd encountered. "Just that I thought about what you said."

He'd said so much to her—uncharacteristically—that he had no idea what she was referring to.

"This afternoon," she clarified.

It hit him then. *Maybe you should think hard about what your life would really be like without her.*

Apparently she had been thinking, if this was her reaction instead of the expected explosion.

"Are you moving in here with us?" Marly asked him, sounding quite open to the idea. He quashed the images that flashed through his mind, and hedged a bit when he answered.

"You'll be seeing me a lot more."

"Where are you gonna sleep?"

It was all Draven could do not to look at Grace. The possibilities that Marly's words brought to mind were vivid and breath-stealing. And he couldn't seem to stop them.

"Outside," he managed to say. "Hear better."

Marly frowned. "Where?"

"On the roof," he said.

And again he didn't dare look at Grace, for fear she might have noticed how gravelly his voice had gone. But he was so focused on not looking at her that the additional words he'd been thinking slipped out aloud.

"For now."

For a third time he didn't dare look at Grace, but he heard her sudden intake of breath. She'd heard, all right. But Marly didn't seem to notice anything unusual. After a moment when she seemed to struggle to take it all in, she turned to face Draven.

"Were they really trying to hurt her?"

Truth, lie or half-truth? The options raced through his mind. But as he stood there, looking at Grace's eyes reproduced in her child's face, he knew there really was only one option.

He nodded.

The girl bit her lip until he could see it turn white where her teeth dug in. "Were they trying to kill her?"

"Maybe. Put her out of commission, most likely."

She absorbed this, pondered for a moment. Then words burst from her, almost explosively.

"Hasn't she been through enough?"

This time he did look at Grace, in time to see a near-startled expression cross her face at her daughter's words. Or at the intensity of them.

"Yes," he said. "She has. That's why we're doing this."

Marly thought about this, too, but not for long. Then she nodded. "All right."

She started toward the bathroom again, then came back and gave her mother a swift hug. Without another word she turned back and continued on her way. When the bathroom door finally closed behind her Draven let out a long, relieved breath.

"Don't know how you do it," he said under his breath.

"It's a challenge," Grace said as if he'd spoken normally, reminding him of the other muttering she'd heard. Those two words that had betrayed the lascivious road his thoughts had barreled down without warning.

He fought down the urge to explain, telling himself nothing he could say could change what she'd heard. Besides, he didn't know what the explanation was, and it didn't seem wise to make something up just now.

"I'm going to go dry my hair," Grace said.

He barely breathed until she was gone into the bedroom, closing the door behind her. Then he let out all the air in his lungs, grateful she'd let the subject drop, that she hadn't called him on his uncharacteristic and no doubt thoroughly unwelcome comment. If there was anyone she'd be less likely to want to share a bed with, he couldn't imagine who it would be.

Maybe her ex-husband, he thought wryly. But nobody else.

A hair-dryer started to hum noisily in the bedroom, joggling him out of his reverie. That had never happened before, either, this drifting off into crazy thoughts about things that he had never dwelt on before. Just another symptom, he told himself, wishing yet again that Josh would have simply let him quit when he'd wanted to instead of pushing until he'd agreed to the bargain that had landed him here. Here, with the one woman he had never been able to forget.

He made himself move, leaving the motor home and heading back over to the trailer. He picked up his bedroll, stuffed his things back in the duffel bag, already planning where he was going to move the motor home.

And wondering, on top of everything else, when he'd become such a coward.

Chapter 11

"That has to be finished by tomorrow. The paving has to start," Grace said into the phone, her voice a bit edgy as she paced.

Draven couldn't hear what was said on the other end of the call, but she was quickly apologetic. "Sorry, Nick. I'm just frustrated."

There was a pause while she listened again. From his seat at the small table, Draven glanced over at the sofa where Marly sat with the control for her video game player in her hands. Her hands were in constant motion, and the images danced across the television screen before her. She had on a headset for the sounds, ordered to do so by Grace so that she could work on the phone.

"I know it's for the best," Grace said into the receiver, "but I don't have to like it. Yes. Tonight's fine for a report." Then, with a grimace, "I'll be here."

She disconnected the call, but kept pacing the floor. She

tapped a finger against the phone receiver as she bit her lip and thought.

Draven yanked his gaze away; the last thing he needed was to watch her nibble on that soft, full lip. It only made him wonder what it would feel like to do it himself. And that idea did things to his gut that he couldn't explain.

After a couple further circuits of the floor, from kitchen to living area and back again, Grace finally tossed the phone down on the counter. It clattered and slid across the granite.

And then she turned on him.

"I hate this!"

"I know," he said quietly.

"How am I supposed to run this project long distance?"

"You're doing fine."

"Fine? Hardly. We're doing concrete, which is a lot different from just rolling out some asphalt. I need to inspect the final grading, check the status on the drainage system, oversee the relocating of the native vegetation, then I—"

He held up a hand, but she was on a roll and it took her a moment to stop.

"Never said you couldn't go out. Just not alone."

"Oh." She sounded a bit deflated, as if she'd been building up to an explosion and felt denied.

"Now?" he asked.

"Yes," she said. Then she glanced at Marly, who was intent on maneuvering some CGI character through a maze, and back at him.

"She'll have to come," he said.

"She'll love that," Grace muttered.

But to his surprise, the girl took the interruption of her play rather quietly. After a heavy sigh, she shut off the game console and the television, pulled on some thick-soled shoes Draven couldn't see how she walked in. Then she stood up, indicating she was ready.

Grace was looking at her daughter warily, as if still awaiting an explosion that hadn't been averted but merely delayed. Draven wondered what it was like to live that way, never knowing if, when or how the explosion would come, or what the trigger would be.

It sounded exhausting.

As they went about Grace's tasks, Draven shifted his mode. Through some strings Josh had pulled—there wasn't a businessman on the planet more respected than he was in law enforcement circles—the Redstone team had been through training given by several federal agencies, including the Secret Service presidential detail. They'd learned about bodyguarding from the best, and they put the knowledge to use on a regular basis. And they'd done well enough that the service had tried to recruit them, even knowing the likelihood of anyone leaving Redstone was slim.

He scanned the area constantly, close in first, then midground, then the perimeter. Anything that moved got attention until identified. If it shouldn't have moved, it got inspected, once turning up a sizable lizard, and once a howler monkey that proceeded to earn its name by chewing him out fiercely for disturbing it.

That at least got Marly to smile. But of course she decided immediately that she wanted it for a pet. Draven told her he wasn't about to catch it, he liked his fingers the way they were. He left it for her mother to talk her out of it; he wouldn't even know where to start. Although he guessed the first night the thing started howling at two in the morning she'd change her mind in a big hurry about its suitability for pethood.

As they crisscrossed the site and covered Grace's list, none of the crew commented on the new arrangements, or on his constant presence, and he wondered if Nick had put the word out. Not that it mattered, really. More eyes the better. It would only make a difference if the problem was inside, and he didn't think it was.

Of course, maybe he just didn't want to believe that, since they'd had so much of that lately. It was a rarity for somebody within Redstone to turn on them; any bad apples usually never made it in, or if they did, were quickly ferreted out.

By the end of the day, Draven realized he had underestimated Grace's stamina. She went from job to job relentlessly, rarely stopping for longer than a minute or two. She also clearly had a tremendous amount of information stored in that clever brain of hers; rarely did she have to consult the clipboard she held for data or dates.

When they got back to the motor home that evening, and Grace had gone to the shower, Draven sat watching Marly start up her video game once more. Watching her much more closely than was necessary, in an effort to keep his mind off of the sound of the shower, and the images the running water brought to his unruly mind.

Watching wasn't enough. Desperate for a stronger distraction, before Marly could turn the game on he asked, "Ever seen your mother at work before?"

"Paperwork, office stuff, yeah. But not like this."

"Pretty impressive."

"She's smart," the girl said with a shrug that said even smart people could be a pain as a parent.

She went back to her game. Draven heard the shower stop, and the door on the other side open as Grace went into the bedroom.

Wrapped in a towel? he wondered.

Naked?

His breath jammed in his throat and stayed there. When he finally remembered how to breathe it was all he could do not to gasp audibly.

Then Marly stopped in her installation and turned to look at him again. It took more effort than he could ever remember having to make to compose his expression. But he did it; the last thing he needed was this child-woman realizing he was sitting here heating up over erotic images of her mother.

"Is it that drug guy?" the girl asked.

He hesitated. Hesitated a moment too long, because Marly flared up at him.

"I'm sick of being treated like I'm a child! Do you think I don't know what really happened out there? That somebody *shot* at her?"

Uh-oh, he thought. "There was no need for you to know, it would only scare you more—"

"Don't *patronize* me! I'm not a baby."

"Never thought you were."

"I don't need to be protected from the truth. I expect that from my mother. She's always been that way, but you're supposed to be some real tough guy. You should be honest, too, but you're as bad as she is."

"Take a breath," he suggested when the tumble of words finally stopped.

She said a word he didn't think girls her age were supposed to know. Then she tossed her game controller on the couch and stomped toward the door.

"Marly," he said warningly.

She ignored him and yanked the door open.

"You're not going anywhere," he told her.

She said that same word again, this time in a physically impossible instruction about what he could do with himself. And started out the door.

He caught her before her foot even hit the first step. His arm around her waist, he swung her off her feet and back into the room. She yelled, and started to struggle. She kicked, and flailed her arms. Landed a couple of glancing blows he barely felt, a couple of solid ones that stung, although he never loosened his grip.

He dragged her back in and shut the door as she screamed at him to let her go.

"Marly!"

His head snapped around at the sound of Grace's wild yell as she came barreling through the bedroom door. She was wielding what looked like a heavy metal flashlight in one hand, clearly ready to use it as a weapon.

Draven froze in an odd sort of awe at the sight of her, all maternal fierceness as she flew to the rescue of her cub. Even Marly went still.

Grace skidded to a halt as she took in the scene. The towel, he thought, almost numbly. It was the towel. She was dressed from the waist down, but a blue towel was still wrapped around her upper body.

The arm holding the flashlight dropped. With the movement, the towel dropped, too. For an instant he caught a glimpse of the ripe, full curve of one breast, tipped with soft pink, before she grabbed the towel and pulled it back into place.

"What's going on?" she demanded.

My blood pressure's going through the roof, for one thing, he thought, listening to his pulse hammering in his ears. That image, that brief flash of feminine flesh, was burned into his memory. He had a feeling he'd be seeing it on an endless loop when he tried to sleep tonight.

This is insane, he thought. He'd seen breasts before. He'd seen them on strangers. On women he was involved with. He'd seen more than just breasts. But nothing had ever affected him the way that split-second glimpse of luscious curve had. Nothing.

"Will you let go *now?*" Marly demanded.

He shook his head as if to clear it, and released her. The girl staggered slightly as her feet hit the floor, righted herself, then spun to glare at him.

"Someone," Grace said, in a voice as grim as any he'd ever heard, "had better start explaining here. Fast."

Marly crossed her arms, still scowling at him, and obviously with no intention of talking. He would have laughed at himself, at his reluctance to face this furious woman, if he hadn't been so busy trying to figure out what to say to her.

"A disagreement about what she needs to know," he finally said. "Made her forget she doesn't go out alone."

Grace's gaze flicked from Draven to her daughter and back. "Need to know what?"

"The truth!" Marly snapped. "You should try it some time."

Grace blinked. "What are you talking about?"

"Nick told me what really happened at the lagoon."

Grace winced. "Oh."

"You didn't think I should know you'd been shot at?"

"I wasn't. It was the truck. The tire."

"Whatever. You could have been killed either way."

"I wasn't."

"So that makes it okay to lie to me?"

"I didn't exactly lie."

"Oh, yeah, like you'd buy that from me."

Draven felt a bit like a spectator at a Ping-Pong match. But he was glad that the girl's resentment had shifted to her mother. Not that he didn't feel sorry for Grace, bearing the brunt of it now, but she at least had practice at it. He had no idea how to handle teenage anger.

"You're right," Grace said. "I wouldn't buy that from you. I apologize."

"Yeah. Well. You should have told me the truth."

"I didn't want to scare you."

Marly glanced at Draven, who had begun to edge slowly backward, toward the door, thinking the last place he wanted to be was in the midst of this family discussion. Especially this female family.

"He said 'need to know,'" Marly said. "Did you ever stop to think that I might *need* to know? What if I saw something, or someone, but I didn't know to say anything?"

She had a point, Draven thought, and he could see Grace realized it, too. Marly glanced at him again before continuing her argument.

"He said 'leverage,' too, that somebody might try to use me on you. What if somebody did, because I didn't know to avoid them, or get away?"

Grace sighed. Her mouth quirked. She looked at Draven. "Don't you just hate it when they're right?"

"Irritating," he acknowledged, barely keeping his mouth from quirking.

"Score!" Marly yelped, as delighted now as she'd been angry before. Draven shook his head, wondering how Grace kept up.

"You two work this out. I'm going to make a call."

He left them there, Grace telling her daughter the whole—well, most, he supposed—of the real story. He stepped outside, relieved to be out of there.

At least, he thought he was relieved. But he had to admit that watching them, and seeing how Marly had reasoned out and won her case, had been oddly pleasing.

As for that glimpse of soft, lush breast, pleasing wasn't the word. It was a very long way past simply pleasing. He was still aching from his response to it, and had the feeling he would be for a long time.

It was going to be a very, very long night.

Chapter 12

Grace rolled over onto her left side. Not that it was going to help, she was sure. Right side or left, back or stomach, covers or none, nothing seemed to matter.

She pounded her pillow into a more comfortable shape, not that she really thought that was going to help, either. She'd gotten close to sleep, repeatedly, so close she could nearly taste the blissful oblivion, but she always jolted wide-awake again before she'd floated away.

Sleep was clearly not on the agenda tonight.

With a sigh she rolled onto her back. She yawned, then listened for any sound from above her, but heard nothing. She'd heard nothing since Draven had climbed up to the roof, reminding her that the sundeck section where he was sleeping was right over her head.

It had to be the stress. Stress over the project, which was normal, stress over the sabotage, which was not. And stress over becoming a target, which most certainly was not. That had to explain why she was in such an uproar.

But it didn't explain why she was so vividly aware of the presence of John Draven, mere feet away, the only thing between them the relatively insubstantial barrier of the motor home's roof.

She felt herself blush in the darkness of the bedroom. She was sure he'd been looking at her when the towel had slipped. She had no idea how much he'd seen, but that he had seen at least a flash, she was sure. And that was certainly more than she was comfortable with.

But she'd been so terrified when she'd heard Marly's scream that she'd reacted instantly and instinctively. Covering up had been the very last thought in her head. Not when her daughter was in danger. She had simply grabbed the nearest thing that could possibly be used as a weapon and run.

She wasn't sure now what she'd thought when she'd raced into the other room of the motor home and seen Draven hanging on to her daughter as she flailed wildly. She remembered noticing that he was doing it easily, despite how strong she knew Marly could be when she was going at full tilt, as she obviously was.

But whatever she'd thought, it hadn't been that her daughter was in any danger. Not from Draven. And the certainty she had about that had surprised her.

With a sigh of surrender she sat up and turned on the bedside light. She'd read her book for a while, she thought. If it didn't hold her interest, then maybe it would put her to sleep.

And maybe it would keep her mind off of the man who was now just above her.

Probably sleeping soundly, she thought wryly.

She picked up the novel she'd purchased in the general store a few days ago. She was so exhausted she couldn't even recall exactly what it was about, so she read the blurb on the back of the thriller again. She wondered if it would live up to the enthusiastic billing.

Generally she was too tired at the end of the day to read more than a page or two, but tonight being tired didn't seem to have much to do with it. With that perversity her mind sometimes had, she couldn't keep her eyes open to read, yet when she again gave up and turned out the light, she still couldn't fall asleep.

She felt an odd sort of hum that seemed to fuzz her head from the ears up, telling her she'd gone beyond mere weariness. Not for the first time she wished the brain came with an off switch.

With your luck, you'd never get it turned back on, she told herself, and flopped back onto her back once more.

She straightened the tangled sheets yet again, then stretched her body as if that would help. She was disconcerted, as she often was, by her brain telling her it was feeling the texture of the sheet against her right foot. It was as real as if the foot were still there, and nothing could convince her brain it wasn't. The therapists and doctors had told her that might never go away, and she wondered how long it would take to stop startling her. She wondered—

A loud, electronic shriek shattered the quiet.

Grace nearly echoed the shriek as she sat bolt upright. Even as she did, she heard a faint scraping sound from the roof, then something hitting the ground beside her window. Draven, she thought, already moving.

"Mom?"

Marly's voice was sleepy and tentative from the other room. Grace rolled out of bed and grabbed her crutch to save time. It could be a weapon, too, if she needed one, she thought as she hurried into the other room.

"I don't know what it was, honey, but I'll find out," she

reassured the girl, who was sitting on the edge of the sofa bed rubbing at her eyes.

"I know what it is," Marly said, then yawned.

Grace stopped in her tracks. "You do?"

The girl nodded. "'S one of those trip wire things we put up. They're alarmed."

"Trip wire?"

Marly explained about the security devices Draven had arranged, sounding rather proud of her part in the setup. Grace hadn't known about that part of it; when Marly had told her they'd set up alarms, she'd not thought of anything that simple.

"I wonder what set it off," Marly mumbled, clearly still groggy with sleep.

"I don't know."

The teenager stood up, gawky and long legged in her rock band T-shirt. "Should we go look?"

Grace nearly gasped aloud at the very idea of her little girl setting out into the night in this foreign place to check out what had set off an alarm of any kind. She wasn't real thrilled about the idea of doing it herself, although she would if she had to.

But she held her tongue for the moment. She and Marly had at last reached a tentative truce last night, after Grace had been as honest as she thought she could be with the girl. And more honest than she'd wanted to be; the urge to protect was very strong. She didn't want to blow that peace now, but there was no way she was letting the girl outside until she knew it was safe.

Which also meant she herself was going to have to stay inside, because if somebody with malicious intent had indeed tripped that wire, she wouldn't leave Marly here by herself.

"Mom? Shouldn't we see what set it off?"

"Mr. Draven's already check—"

She broke off as the sound of the earsplitting claxon halted abruptly. The silence seemed almost eerie after the volume of the noise. She looked at Marly.

"Do they shut off automatically?"

The girl frowned. "I'm not sure. But I don't think so. The wire pulls out a pin, and that sets it off. I think you have to put the pin back in to shut it off."

Which meant that Draven—or somebody—had gotten to where the alarmed trip wire was.

"We'd better go," Marly said. "He's all by himself. If it really is the bad guy, he could get hurt."

"So could you," Grace pointed out, although she was a little concerned herself at the uninterrupted silence.

She told herself firmly that it would take a lot more than one bad guy to seriously hurt John Draven. He'd been a legend at Redstone for longer than she'd been there. His exploits were common knowledge, and he was one of the first things she'd heard about when she'd started her job.

And after the earthquake, she hadn't been at all surprised to learn that the man who had pulled her out, the dark, intense, scarred man who had maimed her in the process of saving her, was the legendary Draven.

"Mom!" Marly said, "you promised not to be so overprotective."

"Stopping you from going out after a possible saboteur who's also possibly armed is hardly being overprotective," Grace said sternly.

"But—"

Grace held up a hand. "Let me get my foot squared away, and if he's not back by then, I'll reconsider."

The girl agreed, reluctantly. So reluctantly that Grace left the bedroom door open as she prepared, so she could hear if her daughter gave in to temptation and the door opened. She dressed quickly, then started on the foot, forgoing the lengthier preparations of lotion and powder in the interest of speed. As time ticked on with no sign of Draven returning, she was getting anxious herself. Or else she was catching Marly's eagerness.

Finished with the foot, she slipped on her other shoe, then stood up, grabbed the flashlight she'd nearly beaned Draven with and headed back into the living room where Marly was impatiently waiting by the door. The moment she saw Grace she reached for the knob.

It turned and the door swung open before she ever touched it. Marly gave a startled exclamation and jumped back. Grace's hand tightened on the flashlight and she started to raise it and step forward.

Draven stepped into the room. In a split second he seemed to assess their relative positions and actions. Grace thought she saw something glitter in his eyes when he looked at her flashlight. But then his gaze settled on Marly. Steadily. Unwaveringly.

"Going somewhere?"

"Mom wouldn't let me go see if you needed help," the girl complained.

"Good," he said.

Marly flushed. She whirled away and flounced down on the rumpled sofa bed. "Fine," she muttered, clearly stung by his words.

Grace thought she heard him draw in a breath. Was dealing with Marly getting to him? When he spoke, his voice was kinder than she had expected.

And it was a complete sentence.

"I need to know if I see someone out there at this hour it's not one of us."

Marly looked up at that. "Oh. Okay, I get it. You don't want to shoot the wrong person."

Another breath. "I don't *want* to shoot anyone."

"Oh." She sounded almost disappointed. After a moment she asked, "What set it off?"

"Your furry buddy."

"What?" Marly frowned, then grinned. "The monkey?"

"None other."

"So this was one of those false alarms you were telling me about?"

"So it seems."

"Well, darn it. I was hoping we'd finally caught the bad guy."

"Me, too," Draven said, making Marly's grin widen.

"Maybe next time," she said, and this time Grace almost grinned at the unsubtle encouraging note in her daughter's voice.

"Maybe." Draven's voice was solemn, and Grace liked him for not laughing.

This time when she went back to bed, Grace expected to be too wound up to sleep. But instead, as if that burst of energy expended when the alarm had sounded had taken the edge off, she was out within moments of her head hitting the pillow. She slipped quickly into a deep sleep, dreamt vividly about things that made no sense but mostly involved the man who had haunted her dreams for months now.

She became restless in the middle of one of these dreams, one in which they'd been alone, and instead of falling the towel she'd had wrapped around her after her shower had simply dissolved into thin air, leaving her breasts bared to a pair of masculine green eyes that, in her deluded state, turned hot with desire. So hot that instead of lifting her hands to cover herself, she straightened her posture, arching her back slightly, as if in the dream she wanted to thrust her breasts toward him. Offer them.

When the trip wire alarm blasted her awake again, she woke up with a cry. She told herself it was merely being startled out of sleep, but some part of her felt a sense of loss that the dream had ended, at that moment.

That realization rattled her so much that it took her a moment to focus on what was happening outside her too-erotic dreamworld.

Be glad it ended before the rejection, she thought, and forced herself to concentrate on reality.

Had she heard Draven leaving the roof again? She couldn't be sure; she'd been too soundly asleep and too slow to wake up to know if she'd heard those sounds again. But she knew Marly would be awake again, and she wasn't confident enough that Draven's words had taken to simply trust her not to do anything foolish.

Once more she got up and put herself back together, telling herself that she was going to start sleeping with the prosthetic foot on if this kept up.

And dressed, she added to herself as she pulled off her sleep shirt, which reminded her of the dream and sent a fierce blast of heat through her that made her sway slightly. Her nipples tightened at the memory of that vivid image, and she ached in a way she never had before.

It scared her, and she made herself hurry to finish and get out to Marly.

The girl was huddled by the door, but she hadn't gone out. She glanced up as her mother came in.

"Bet it's the monkey again," Marly said.

"Most likely," Grace agreed; at this point she'd go along with anything that would keep the girl safely inside the motor home.

They hovered near the door, wondering what was going on out there. And Grace had to admit she didn't like sitting back and waiting for the big, strong man to handle this. It wasn't in her nature. She was an expert in a field that was dominated by men, and while she always tried to get along, she had never deferred to them.

Unless, of course, they knew more than she did. She was confident, but not stupid.

And Draven, she thought, knew a heck of a lot more about what to do out there than she would ever know. More than she ever wanted to know.

Once she remembered that, she felt herself calm slightly. He was the expert, and by all accounts one of the best in the world at what he did. He would handle this, and he didn't need any help from her, and he certainly didn't need any interference from a teenage girl. His job was to protect the project, and by circumstance he'd gotten pulled into protecting them as well. So while he was doing the first, the least she could do was help with the second.

"Boy, he's not getting much sleep tonight, is he?"

Grace looked at her daughter. "No. No, he's not."

In fact, now that she thought about it, he probably hadn't gotten much rest since he'd been here. She knew he spent a lot of the night watching the surveillance monitors, so he was starting out at a loss. When he did sleep, at first he'd been in the construction trailer, on the floor. Then on the roof of the trailer, and now on the roof of the motor home. Hardly conducive to sound sleep.

Of course, that was probably why he was doing it. She'd bet he didn't want to get too comfortable, for fear he'd miss something, some sound, or movement, or like the other night, the smell of danger.

"Mom?"

She snapped out of her reverie and looked at her daughter. "What?"

"Did you know him before he came here?"

Grace tensed. She'd never told her daughter exactly what

had happened during and after the earthquake. Marly had been staying with Grace's aunt Charlotte during that time, since Grace hadn't wanted to take her to a part of the world that wasn't the most stable. So by the time Redstone had flown her home to the States, she'd buried the incident in her mind while she concentrated on her rehab.

She looked at the girl, who met her gaze steadily. Grace remembered her daughter's plea to be told the truth, remembered that she'd had some very good reasons for it.

Perhaps she had a right to know this, as well.

"Mr. Draven is the man who pulled me out of that building after the earthquake."

Marly's eyes widened and her mouth opened in shock. "He's the guy? Why didn't you tell me?"

"I try not to think about it very often," Grace said. It was the honest truth; until Draven had shown up here she spent a great deal—probably too much—of her energy every day not thinking about it.

And then he'd arrived, and it had become impossible. His presence was just too big, too much, she simply couldn't ignore him. He took up too much space, too much air.

He was too...too, she thought.

"Well, yeah," Marly said, "but, jeez, I wish I'd known."

"Why?" she asked, curious.

"I woulda been nicer, maybe."

Well, hallelujah, Grace thought.

"How come he's not friendlier to you?" Marly asked.

"I don't know. I think that's just the way he is, that's his nature." She thought about it a moment, then wondered aloud, "Or maybe not. I suppose it's possible that I'm not a very enjoyable memory for him, either."

"Why? I'd think saving somebody's life would make you feel good."

"I'm sure it does. But in some cases there's a downside,

too. Sometimes to save someone you have to do things that aren't pleasant."

Marly frowned. "You mean your foot? But why would that bother him? I mean, if he got you out in time, before the building—" The girl stopped suddenly, and her eyes got huge once again. "Oh, wow. Your foot…"

Grace looked at her, not denying or confirming the implication, wondering if there was a way to continue to avoid this.

"He did it?" Marly asked, her voice barely above a whisper. "He cut it off, right there?"

Grace sighed. She'd never told the girl, knew she'd always assumed her foot had had to be amputated later on in the hospital. She hadn't felt it necessary to correct that impression, in fact had chosen not to, to avoid giving the child any more nightmares than she was already having. But now she didn't seem to have any choice; it was the truth or a face-to-face lie.

"There was no choice. It was the only way to get me out in time. He knew the building was about to collapse. That we had only minutes. Maybe seconds."

Marly shivered as she stared at her mother.

Now that she'd started, Grace decided she might as well finish. "He risked his own life. He would have been killed, too, if that building had come down. But he stayed, to get me out."

"No wonder you seem so twitchy around him. Now I understand."

You only think you do, Grace thought, fighting down the rush of color that threatened to flood her face as the memory of her dreams came back to her when Marly said the word *twitchy.* That was a good description of it. She was twitchy, all right, but it had nothing to do with her foot. And everything to do with the man who had separated her from it.

She told herself it was only natural, to feel, or imagine you felt, some sort of attraction to the man who'd saved your life. That's all it was.

"And now I understand why he's so weird around you," Marly said.

Grace fought down the wave of aching sensation and focused on her daughter. "What?"

"He must really feel like crap, having to do that to you."

Grace was so startled by the idea her daughter expressed that she neglected to object to the language. She had never thought of that, never thought it was even possible. Draven seemed so invulnerable, impervious to the frailties that plagued ordinary mortals.

She couldn't believe that, however bloody and awful what he'd done to her might have been, that he hadn't seen and done worse in his years with Redstone, or with the military before that. Something had to have put that look in his eyes, the look that chilled even the coldest of souls. You didn't get that way by growing daffodils.

"I sort of doubt he feels that badly about it," she said. "As I said, there was no choice."

"I'll bet he does," Marly insisted. "I bet it gives him nightmares, just like us."

Grace tilted her head to look at Marly. "You still have nightmares?"

That shrug again. And an embarrassed expression as she muttered, "Sometimes."

The girl had never admitted to that before. Grace was fairly certain she'd had some nasty dreams, as she herself had, after she'd first arrived home. Too many times she'd found the girl up walking around at odd hours of the night. And her bed had been a tangled wreck in the mornings, as if she had tossed and turned all night.

But Marly had always denied it, insisted she was fine,

with that affected, blasé attitude of the young teenager. Grace hadn't believed it at the time, and had kept watching her daughter carefully. The nighttime excursions and restlessness seemed to have eased as time passed, but still—

This time it wasn't the alarm that split the nighttime quiet.

It was a shot.

Chapter 13

He didn't come back.

Grace stared at the door as if she could make it swing open by sheer force of will.

"Mom?"

Marly was sounding more upset with every query. But she couldn't leave the girl alone, not with somebody out there with a gun.

Of course, it could have been Draven, shooting. Despite his comment to Marly about not wanting to shoot anyone, she was certain he would do whatever was necessary. She was a little surprised at how much faith she had in that, but there it was. She supposed all that telling herself he had the reputation he had for a reason had finally sunk in.

"It's his job, Marly. He's the expert."

"What good does that do if somebody gets the drop on him?"

At the phrase Grace reminded herself to more carefully monitor her daughter's choices in entertainment.

"Being the expert is what keeps that from happening," she said.

"But what if that shot was at him? Like…like a…a sniper or something!" Marly, not having her mother's knowledge of who and what Draven was, asked anxiously. "What if he's out there hurt, bleeding, maybe even dying?"

Grace had to admit her daughter's frightened words sent some ugly images through her head. But she couldn't quite wrap her mind around the idea of the mighty John Draven being taken down like that.

But, once again she had a point. The bad guys could always get lucky, she thought. It happened. Cops got shot all the time, even with all their training.

"Mom, come on!" Marly was nearly shouting now.

"You heard what he said," Grace said, afraid the girl was going to bolt in a moment. "He has to know anybody moving is the bad guy."

"You think half the crew isn't out there after hearing a shot?"

Grace stared at her daughter. When had she gotten so logical? And when had she herself apparently lost the capacity to think clearly? At least, when it came to Draven.

Probably the moment he stepped off that plane, she muttered inwardly.

"You're right," she said aloud, earning a flash of a smile from Marly. "But we're going to stay in the main quad until we find out what's going on. No straying out to the edge, even though that's where the trip wires are. All right?"

Marly hesitated, but then nodded.

She had been right, Grace realized, soon after they stepped outside. Several outside lights were now on, in addition to the high-intensity spots over the heavy equipment enclosure that were always on all night. And she could see men moving in and out of the pools of light.

"Over there," Grace said, pointing to where a silhouette against the brighter lights appeared to be Nick. "Let's go see what he knows."

Marly grudgingly followed her, muttering all the way that they should be out looking for Draven instead. Grace registered this, and wondered when the man had become so important to the girl, despite their disagreements. For a guy who insisted he knew nothing about kids, he'd certainly made an impression on this one. Perhaps she was the one who should be learning from him when it came to relating to her daughter.

"Hell of a way to wake up in the middle of the night," Nick said when he saw Grace approaching. "Oops," he added when he saw Marly behind her. "Sorry."

"Don't apologize. It seems she has her own vocabulary to apologize for," Grace said dryly.

"Yeah, yeah," Marly muttered. "Where's Draven?"

"Mr. Draven," Grace corrected automatically.

"Yesterday he said to call him Draven," Marly protested.

"Haven't seen him yet," Nick said, cutting off the incipient argument. "Must be out prowling around."

She glanced at Marly, then asked Nick, "You don't think he might be hurt? That shot…"

"Nah. He's the toughest man I've ever met. He knows his stuff. If anybody's hurt out there, I'd lay odds it's the guy behind all this nuisance."

"How can you be sure?" Marly asked.

Nick looked at the girl. "Honey, that man went into the jungle of Nicaragua and pulled out some warlord's prime prisoner, all by himself. You think he can't handle some two-bit drug dealer's flunky?"

Marly stared at Nick. "He did?"

"And single-handedly rescued the entire Redstone staff when some extremist in the Philippines grabbed them to try to blackmail Josh into using his influence to get their friends out of jail."

The girl was gaping now, like a youngster who has just gotten the first glimpse of a much bigger, wider world than was encompassed in her own narrow view.

Grace knew Nick had been telling those tales to reassure Marly, but in the process he'd managed to reassure her a bit as well. But as long as there was no sign of Draven, she wasn't going to be certain he was all right.

It was only natural that she feel disturbed, she told herself. After all, the man was part—a very big part, much bigger than she herself—of Redstone, and they truly were all one family. And he'd come here to protect her project, so of course she felt guilty that he might be hurt in the process.

Not to mention the fact that she owed him her life. How could she not be upset at the prospect?

"You and the crew stick close by here until we know for sure. I don't want anybody...getting hurt," Grace told him, first hesitating, then omitting the phrase "anybody else."

"Yes, ma'am," Nick said, a bit fervently. "I'm not big on getting shot at."

Grace looked at Marly. "Let's go over to the trailer. You're good with those security monitors and recordings, let's see if we can see anything."

Brightening at the prospect and, Grace hoped, at the compliment, Marly nodded quickly and started that way. Grace followed this time, vaguely aware that her leg was protesting the extra time on her feet tonight. She was comfortable with the prosthetic, but that didn't mean the stump of her leg had completely toughened up yet. She might have to give it a rest if this kept up.

Marly trotted up the trailer steps and opened the door.

"Hey!" the girl yelped.

Fear shot through Grace. She leapt up the two steps in one move, landing on the artificial foot. Ignoring the pain that stabbed through her leg, she yanked Marly back.

And then she saw what had startled the girl.

Draven.

Alive, well and sitting at the monitors calmly scanning recorded images.

Draven had turned when he'd heard the noises outside, hand reaching for the weapon at the small of his back. It was probably just Nick, he'd seen the lights go on over there, but he wasn't big on taking anything for granted. It was one reason he was still alive.

When he saw who was there, he realized he shouldn't be surprised. He should have known the girl wouldn't be able to stay put forever with all this activity going on.

When Grace pulled the girl aside and put herself in front of her, he was puzzled for a moment.

When Grace swore at him, something he'd never heard her do despite provocation, he was more than puzzled, he was startled.

"I don't think my mother would appreciate the characterization," he said mildly.

"Then she should have taught you better manners!"

"Grace—"

"Did it never occur to you that we all heard that shot?"

"Of course—"

"Or that none of us knew where you were?"

"The alarm—"

She swore at him a second time. "Damn it, Draven, we didn't know if you were lying out there bleeding to death or what!"

He blinked. "Me?"

"Even the great Draven isn't invulnerable," she snapped. "For all we knew, that shot had hit you. For all we knew, you were dead."

"Not likely," he said, more than a little stunned by the turn this had taken.

Grace stared at him. High emotion was roiling in her eyes, and he wasn't sure why. There was a trace of lingering fear, yes, but any mother would feel that way, wouldn't they, hearing a shot and having their child in the vicinity?

He couldn't think of any other explanation for her state. Of course, he could barely think at all, looking at her. The only thing that was clear in his mind was that Grace, angry, was the most incredible thing he'd ever seen in his life. He told himself it was because he knew up close and personal how close she'd come to dying, that seeing her so alive and vibrant now was just a spectacular comparison.

But on some level, someplace buried deep inside, he knew better. He knew it was more than that. Knew there was something within him responding to her in a way he'd never felt before. He knew it. Just like he knew he could never acknowledge that fact.

At a loss for what else to do, he tried to reassure her. "It would take more than a guy with lousy aim and a popgun to do any real damage."

She continued to stare. Then, when she finally spoke again, he winced inwardly.

"Kryptonite?" she suggested, in that sweet voice that he'd learned meant it was time to tread very carefully.

Marly giggled, taking the edge off the confrontation.

"I never said I was a superhero." His voice sounded stiff even to his own ears.

"Contrary to your reputation?" Grace said, her voice still carrying that tone that made him wary.

Draven wasn't sure what to say. After a moment's pondering he decided the best course was to say nothing just now. Let her take the lead, answer only what he had to and hope she calmed down. He wasn't sure exactly what had her so wound up anyway.

"What happened?" Marly asked. "Was it the bad guy this time?"

With a wary glance at Grace, Draven answered her. "It was somebody. The alarm scared him off."

"Did you hit him?"

He frowned at the girl's obvious enthusiasm. "I never got close enough to even throw a punch."

"I meant shoot him," Marly explained.

"Sorry to disappoint," he said, "I never drew my weapon."

"Oh."

She did sound disappointed. Again. He guessed he just wasn't living up to her image. But there really had been no point in trying to shoot back when the man had fired at him. Besides the fact that he didn't want to start a running gun battle here on the site. He preferred to choose his own ground for that kind of thing.

He'd heard the round whistle past his ear. Realized right away that if he'd ducked left instead of right, he'd likely be dead, a round buried somewhere in his head. He'd wondered if the shooter was that good, or just lucky. Logic told him if it was somebody connected to *el mercader,* it was skill. If not, all bets were off, it could go either way.

Crouching below the level of the brush, he had worked his way toward the hollow he thought the shot had come from. He had a feeling the shooter was long gone, that the round he'd capped off had been more warning than anything else, but that was another thing he didn't take for granted.

"Did you see him?" Grace asked.

"Not well," he said. "Enough to see he was male, thin and

wiry. Not too tall, maybe five-eight or nine. But I got a look at his car."

"What was it?"

He looked at her, a vision of her finding it and confronting the driver shooting through his mind and making him cringe inwardly.

"You've got to promise—both of you—" he added with a glance at Marly "—that if you see it you do *nothing*. You let me know and you stay away. Period. No exceptions. And that goes for the crew, too. I don't want anybody getting hurt here."

"Yeah, yeah," Marly muttered.

"She promises," Grace said. "And so do I. Nick will get the word to the crew."

After a moment, Draven realized he had little choice. The more eyes looking for this guy, the quicker they'd find him.

"Light-colored four-door, maybe off-white or a light yellow. American make. Older, kind of beat-up, with big, square taillights. Got a clatter in the engine, like it's got a bad valve."

And he would remember the sound if he ever heard it again. He'd listened to it pull away, his eyes closed to concentrate on the sound, committing the sour note to memory. He had a good ear for machinery, and knew he'd recognize it.

"Did you get the license?" Marly asked excitedly.

"Partial," Draven said, stifling the twitch of his lips at her enthusiasm. "There was some mud on the plate, covering a couple of the numbers."

"Can you still check it, like the cops do? And find out who owns it?"

"It's harder with only a partial, but it can be done." His mouth quirked. "But there aren't that many cars on the island in the first place. Be faster to just look for it."

"Oh." Again that disappointment in the girl's voice. But

Draven didn't mind; at least things had calmed down. Enough that he felt safe in pointing out that they weren't supposed to go anywhere without him.

"But you were gone," Marly said in response. "How could we go with you?"

Now there was teenage logic, Draven thought. "You weren't supposed to go at all," he said.

"But we were worried," Marly pointed out in turn.

"You both were safest staying in the motor home."

"Us?" Marly scowled at him. "You are *so* dense!"

He drew back slightly, wondering what had brought that assessment on.

"Did it never occur to you," Marly asked, in a startlingly adult-sounding voice, "that it was *you* we were worried about?"

Something slammed into his chest with the force of a fist. "Me?" he asked.

Or tried to, the word came out very oddly, almost like a startled squeak. He looked at Grace, who was watching him steadily. He saw something in her eyes that tightened the knot that was making it hard to breathe.

"Is it that strange," she asked softly, "to think somebody might actually worry about you?"

Yes, was the answer that came to his lips, but he bit it back. It sounded too damned pitiful.

"Don't worry about me. It's my job." He managed to keep his voice fairly level.

"They're not mutually exclusive," Grace said.

"They should be," he said, not liking how gruff he sounded, but seemingly he'd lost control over that, too.

He didn't want to think that simply coming here and facing the woman who haunted him—for he'd finally had to admit to himself that it was Grace herself who haunted him, not what he'd had to do to her—had so shaken him. Didn't want to admit she had that much power over him. Especially knowing she had never intentionally done a thing to wield that power. Probably didn't even know she had it.

How could she know? To her, he was eternally connected to her nightmare, what had to be the worst trauma of her life. How could she know, and why would she care if she did know, that it haunted him, too? What right did he have to be preoccupied about it? It was her body, her life that had been irrevocably changed. He'd walked away, as he had countless times before.

Only now was he facing the possibility that while he might have walked away, he'd never really left it behind.

And for the first time in his life and career, he wanted to quit in the middle of a job.

Chapter 14

Draven had changed, somehow.

Grace considered this as she looked at him across the motor home's table. Marly was in the bathroom, where she was sure the girl would take at least an hour on her new, experimental beauty regimen. It tugged at her heart; her little girl was growing up. And it was going to be a battle, the wisdom of age combating the ignorance of youth, bouncing her back and forth between near-adult acumen and childish lack of judgment.

But she had to go through it, and there was nothing Grace could do about it except be there. So she turned back to the silent man sitting across the table. This had become somewhat of a routine since that day at the lagoon; she would get up, fix coffee, and the smell drew him in.

There was something different about him since last night, when the alarms had sounded. It wasn't anything obvious, anything she could pinpoint. He went about his work as before—and still not sleeping enough, she thought—and acted the same as he always had.

But there was something in the way she would catch him looking at her, watching, as if she were…something he was trying to figure out.

When he'd first arrived it had been painful just to look at him, to see that rough, angular, scarred face and remember the first time she'd seen it, looming over her, at that moment the most welcome sight in the world. Her salvation, her deliverance from death. And then the dispenser of agony.

Now, if she was honest, she'd have to admit part of the difficulty of having him here was based in the attraction she felt. *And because you're embarrassed to even look at him, after that dream you had,* she told herself sourly.

She looked out the window and somewhat wistfully remembered the time when she'd been free to come and go as she pleased. And how it felt to not be worrying about the job, a constant concern now.

She didn't think she'd made a sound, but he looked up from the cup of coffee he held. It was still the strongest stuff she'd ever tasted, but she supposed he needed it that way to keep going as he did. She'd have been facedown in the dirt long before now. But it was starting to show, she thought. Finally. His eyes were as vivid and alert and wary as ever, but there were shadows beneath them, painted there by the lack of sleep.

When she poured her own coffee, she only poured a half a cup and then diluted it with hot water to make it drinkable. He'd told her she didn't need to make it stronger for him, he appreciated her simply making it. But it was easy enough to doctor her own, and she felt it was the least she could do.

She heard the shower start, and knew her daughter would be in there until the hot water ran out. And now, she knew, was her chance to bring up what had been bothering her ever since Marly had said it.

"May I ask you something, about that day in Turkey?"

He didn't move, but somehow she thought he'd tensed. She picked her next words carefully.

"Does that day…bother you?"

He looked up then. "Bother me?" He gave a short, hard laugh. "Bother isn't the word I'd use, no."

She had to know if Marly's theory was wrong—she didn't think she could bear to make a fool out of herself by assuming he even thought about that day much at all.

"What word would you use?"

He held her gaze for a long moment. Her heart started to pick up speed, and she wasn't even sure why. She thought she saw hints of a battle taking place in his head, and wondered if it was some very rare moment when he let something show, or if she was possibly getting better at reading him.

"Please," she said. "It's important to me."

A muscle in his jaw jumped. She tried not to read too much into it, tried not to think that it really meant so much to him that he couldn't speak of it.

"Haunt," he finally said.

She sucked in a breath. Marly had been right. "Surely you've seen worse things."

He nodded. "And done worse. But never to a civilian, an innocent."

She got up then. She faced him, standing tall and straight, her head up. "I'm standing here, alive and well," she said with emphasis on the last word, "because of you."

"Ian Gamble," he said.

"Yes, him, too, but if not for you, I wouldn't have been around to try out his new foot. I wouldn't be here at all."

He gave that half shrug again, as if he were very uncomfortable with the turn this had taken.

"Grace—"

"No, let me finish. I know there was no other choice. I understand that." She paused, to let him know she knew there was a big difference, then she added firmly, "I *believe* that."

He was staring at her. And she saw in those green eyes that *haunt* was indeed the word; it was as if she could see a string of countless nights fraught with images as ugly as her own.

"How can you do that?" he said at last, and there was an undertone in his voice that she'd never heard before. It sounded almost like wonder. "I cut into your living flesh, sawed off a part of your body, caused you horrific pain and hardship for the rest of your life."

"You may not believe this, but it's truly not like that anymore. There are so many who are worse off. I kept my knee, do you have any idea how important that is?"

He shook his head, slowly. "I maimed you and you're… absolving me? Forgiving me?"

It was worse than she'd feared, Grace thought. She spoke quickly, putting all the sincerity she felt into her words.

"There's nothing to forgive. You didn't cause any of what happened. You only did what had to be done. If you hadn't, I'd be dead. I would never see my daughter grow up, and she would be stuck for the rest of her life with only a father who didn't want her."

He lowered his eyes then, staring into his coffee cup. She thought she heard a breath escape him. This was more emotion than she'd ever seen from the man, and it was rattling her almost as much as it was apparently rattling him. She took another deep breath and let the words unroll.

"I can't say I don't have painful memories, that you're not connected to them. No, I'm not the same woman I was, and perhaps there's not a man on the planet who can look past the physical change, but that's all right. I don't need that. I

love my work, my daughter and my life. That's more than
many have. And it's thanks to you that I have any of it. So I
wanted you to know how grateful I am."

He was looking at her as if shell-shocked. His expression
alone told her how much he had assumed about what she felt
about what he'd had to do. If she'd realized, she would have
done this much sooner.

And it both amazed her and gave her hope that it had been
her little girl who had figured it out.

Draven went from camera three to camera four, checking for any problems. This was his second trip, because
he didn't trust himself. He'd made two circuits of the
perimeter, too, because he'd repeatedly caught himself off
in the ozone somewhere, and right now he didn't trust his
autopilot.

He wasn't often shocked. Or stunned. Grace O'Conner
had done both.

Hell, she'd blown him away.

He knew he would never forget the way she'd stood there
and given him total absolution. His head had known what
she'd said was true; it had been the only thing to do, but he
had never expected her to see it that way. He'd expected to
be the star in her nightmares for the rest of her life.

When she'd seemed to relax a little around him, he'd assumed it was simply practice, that since he'd practically
taken up residence she'd gotten used to him. He'd never
considered that she actually might not hate him for what had
happened that day in Turkey.

. And now he was reeling. Because now, without the buffer
of the negative feelings he'd assumed she had, he had to
admit she'd gotten to him. Gotten to him as no one ever had,
in a very personal way.

He stopped in his tracks as a stunning thought hit him.

Once again what Josh had said came back to him. *Handle whatever you find—no matter what it is.*

Draven had thought at the time there'd been an odd sort of emphasis on those particular words. He hadn't known why then, but now he was wondering if somehow, in that amazing way Josh had of reading people, he'd known something. If he'd sent Draven here on purpose, knowing Grace was here. If he'd sent him here to deal with the demons he hadn't even known the source of himself. If that was what Josh had meant when he'd said only he could handle this.

He wouldn't put it past his boss to have done just that. It was just the kind of thing Josh Redstone would do. He'd have to have a word with him when he finished here. Asking him for help was one thing, manipulating him was something else again, something he didn't take kindly to.

He filed away the notion and went back to work. He checked the mount on the camera closest to the water, making sure it wasn't damaged from the salt spray and air. He gave it much more attention than necessary, trying to divert his thoughts. He felt as if his mind was working at triple speed, as if too many thoughts and images were careening around inside his skull, bouncing off each other and the walls and never slowing down enough for him to catch and process them.

He was not used to feeling like this. About anything. That it was a woman shook him. He'd been attracted to women over the years, had occasionally acted on the feeling. But the bottom line was still that he'd never met a woman he couldn't leave behind.

And I sure as hell don't want to start now, he thought. Especially a woman with a child he could barely deal with.

As if any woman would take you on in the first place, he reminded himself.

The two serious relationships—God, he hated that word—he'd ever had had both ended for the same reason: neither woman could deal with his work. Whether it was the work itself, and the demands it made, or the fact that it was his first priority, he didn't know. Probably both, he thought as he finally moved on to the next camera.

Or maybe it was simply him. There was no denying he was no prize for any woman. He had few illusions about himself. He knew he was a loner, a hard case, blunt, pragmatic to the extreme, with far too many rough edges. And his job meant long hours and lots of travel, was sometimes risky and a few times deadly.

But above all, he knew he didn't have a romantic bone in his battle-scarred body. And Grace deserved the exact opposite of all he was—and wasn't. She was gutsy, smart and beautiful, and many other things he admired. More woman than a man like him had any right to.

He nearly groaned that he was even thinking about such things. But how could he not, after what she'd said?

…perhaps there's not a man on the planet who can look past the physical change.

Didn't she know how beautiful she was? Still was, no matter what had happened? Didn't she know that her missing foot was nothing when the rest was so beautiful and the brain was quick and sharp enough to keep any man working all the time just to keep up? That her courage dealing with what had happened to her made her even more incredible, more sexy?

Heat shot through him, a stabbing, piercing claw making his body clench until he almost doubled over. He nearly gasped at the force of it. It had been a very, very long time since he'd wanted, truly wanted. Hell, he wasn't sure he'd ever wanted like this. And was even less sure that he was going to be able to keep it under control. He had the feeling he was going to be glad there was a teenager around to force him to keep a leash on this ferocious need. Because he had to keep it leashed. Just because she'd forgiven him didn't mean Grace would have any interest at all in getting involved with the chaos that was his life. And his mind. And the emotions he didn't want to admit to even having.

Yeah, you're a pretty messed up package, he thought wryly.

He forced himself to pay attention to the matter at hand. He needed to be doubly sure everything was in place and working. Whoever it was, Draven didn't think their culprit was going to give up easily.

He wanted to adjust the outer perimeter cams; the recorded visuals at the time of the alarm trip had shown only a shadowy figure with some sort of hat pulled down and hiding his features. When he'd tripped the wire and the alarm sounded, he'd jumped, startled, and the hat had flown off. He'd grabbed it and run, which was why he was already getting into the car when Draven had gotten there.

He might need to install some floods, at least on the perimeter cams, he thought. The extra light would have made this guy plainly visible. He'd have somebody send them out. If he'd thought of it earlier, he could have had them come along with the other delivery he was expecting.

Which reminded him to check the time, and he glanced at his watch. The boat should be reaching them any time now. He picked up the pace and finished his inspection, better able to concentrate now that he had a reason to hustle. Then he headed down to the dock.

He wanted to make this pickup himself, so he could go over the situation thoroughly, but didn't want to leave Grace and Marly unguarded for too long. With a little luck, no one else would notice the arrival for a while, and he could still get the briefing done.

When he was within sight of the cove, he saw that Jorge Nunez and his offshore racer were already in sight. By the time he got down to the pier, the powerful boat had slowed and was sliding neatly toward the docking area. Draven walked down to meet it, and when Nunez tossed him the mooring lines, he tied them neatly off on the cleats bolted to the pier decking.

Nunez waved as his passenger bent to grab up a duffel bag that looked much like Draven's own.

"On my way to Ambergris," the man in the captain's hat said, referring to Ambergris Cay, the largest and most developed island off Belize's coast.

"I have a charter out to the reef. A load of divers, very rich," Nunez added with a grin.

That would make it a profitable afternoon, Draven thought; Belize's reef was the second largest in the world, after Australia, and you could spend hours there without realizing. He nodded in understanding that the man was, for once, on a schedule, but kept his eyes on the young man who tossed the duffel bag onto the pier and leapt fairly agilely up after it.

Once he was on the pier, Draven freed the bowline. Without prompting, the young man did the same with the stern. Nunez waved again and was off, leaving a swirling wake behind him and kicking up a rooster tail of spray to mark his course.

The new arrival held out his hand. "Mr. Draven."

Draven shook hands briefly, noting the grip was strong but not challenging.

Kieren Buckley looked much as Draven had remembered from his Redstone interview. Only slightly shorter than he himself, lean but muscular, with sandy-brown hair he wore in a buzz cut that reminded Draven of his own service days. He had the small goatee that seemed to come standard with twentysomethings these days, sparse enough that Draven thought he'd look better without it.

But what Draven had noticed first about him was his eyes. Not the color, which was an amber sort of brown, but the calm alertness in them, and in his entire stance. He'd clearly been nervous about the interview, but he'd met Draven's eyes steadily, and that was a make or break point with the head of Redstone Security.

"You made good time," Draven said.

"Yes, sir. Went like clockwork."

"Redstone," Draven answered simply.

"Yeah, I'm beginning to see that."

"You finish reading the file?"

He nodded. "On the plane."

"Good. Ready?"

"Absolutely. Thanks for asking for me."

Draven gave him a sideways look. "St. John tell you what the job was?"

Buckley nodded.

"That doesn't bother you?"

"No, sir. I'm sure there's a reason, or you wouldn't be asking."

He could have been sucking up, but Draven didn't think so. And Redstone people always got the benefit of the doubt, even the new ones.

"Doesn't hurt to be in paradise, either?" Draven suggested.

Buckley shrugged. "I'm a cool-weather, mountain kind of guy myself, but this is nice for a change. What's the setup here?"

"Redstone owns the south two-thirds of the island. Matola City, such as it is, is about two miles north. At the far north tip of the cay is a guy you'll need to know about, but we'll get into that later."

Buckley nodded. "What's first?"

Draven's mouth quirked. "You meet the family," he said. "I'll fill you in as we go."

He led the way, giving Buckley the layout of the site as they went, pointing out the various work and storage areas, and the construction trailer. He told him about the situation up until now, including Grace's close encounter with the enemy.

"She's the one who got hurt in that earthquake in Turkey, isn't she?"

"Yes," Draven said succinctly.

"I heard about her. Guess she's one tough lady."

You don't know the half of it, kid. "She is," he said.

When they got to the motor home, he knocked. Marly pulled open the door.

"Mom's in the…"

Her voice trailed away as she spotted the man with him. Her young face betrayed her every thought as she gaped at the handsome young man.

That should keep you occupied, young lady, Draven thought, with no small amount of satisfaction that his choice had had the desired effect. He'd figured a girl Marly's age couldn't help but react like this to the good-looking kid only ten years older than she was. When he'd made the call to Redstone headquarters, he'd intended to just let St. John decide who to send, but then he'd remembered the young man he'd personally interviewed, and made his own selection.

"Hi," Buckley said. "You must be Marly."

Apparently dumbstruck, the girl just stared at him. Finally she managed to nod.

Buckley jerked a thumb at Draven. "He didn't tell me you were cute."

The girl's color deepened and her eyes went even wider. *Smooth,* Draven thought. *This just might work better than I'd even hoped.*

"I…what…who are you?" Marly finally managed to ask.

"I'm Kieren Buckley," he said cheerfully, with a grin that made the girl blush. "I'm your new babysitter."

Chapter 15

"He's what?" Grace asked.

"He's going to watch out for Marly. She's his only assignment."

Grace looked dubiously at the young man her daughter was talking to so fervently, a few yards away. To her he looked barely older than the fourteen-year-old herself.

"What is he? Sixteen?"

Draven's mouth quirked. Either he was relaxing, Grace thought, or she really was learning to read his slight expression changes.

"He's twenty-four," he said.

She barely managed not to gape at him. "Twenty-four? That's twenty-four?" She felt ancient, looking at him and realizing he was ten years older than Marly.

"The older you get, the younger they look," Draven said as if he'd read her thoughts. She couldn't tell if he'd been teasing or simply voicing an observation; his voice was dead-pan, as was his face.

"He's a trained Redstone agent," Draven said, obviously trying to reassure her. "And if it makes you feel better, he was also a cop in L.A. for a couple of years."

"Why did he leave?"

"That's his to share or not. I can only tell you it wasn't anything negative. He wasn't fired, asked to leave or guilty of any misconduct."

"Oh." She eyed the new arrival warily, then looked back at Draven. "I can trust him with her?"

"You can."

"You know what I mean?" she asked, not certain if he understood all the ramifications of entrusting a fourteen-year-old girl to a young man she'd never met. A very handsome young man.

"Yes. He's completely trustworthy. In all areas."

She considered this for a moment. Then realized if Kieren Buckley was Redstone security, he'd been vetted within an inch of his life. The L.A.P.D. background check likely paled in comparison to what Redstone put him through.

She looked over at the pair again, thinking she'd never seen her daughter blush so much. And she was actually giggling. Marly was not just laughing, but giggling, in a girly sort of way Grace couldn't remember ever having heard from her daughter before.

Grace's mouth twisted into a wry smile. "He's too darn cute. Every adolescent girl's dream. She's going to get a crush on him."

"I'm counting on it."

Grace's head snapped around. "What?"

"I'm counting on it," he repeated. "Better chance she'll cooperate, stay with him."

Grace stared at him. "And stay safe," she said softly.

He nodded.

She shook her head in wonder. "Don't ever tell me again you don't understand teenagers."

"I don't. But I've seen the reaction he gets."

"From girls?"

"Women, too."

She glanced back over at the two, this time studying Kieren's perfect features. "Too pretty for me," she said.

When she turned back, Draven was studying her intently. She felt a blush rising to her own cheeks as she realized that could have been interpreted as expressing a preference for more rugged looks.

Looks, for example, like his.

Well, it's true, she admitted inwardly. *You've never been attracted to the pretty ones.*

And Draven was many things; strong, powerful, mysterious, scarred, competent and tough, but there was no way you could call him pretty. Not even good-looking, that was too bland. He was much more than that.

She thought for a moment, trying to come up with the right word, and nearly blushed again when the only term that came to mind was *magnificent.* But she wasn't sure that wasn't the perfect description.

"I would give a great deal," he said in a voice so soft it wouldn't carry beyond her ears, "to know what you're thinking right now."

Caught, Grace lost the battle with the rising blush, and felt the heat of color flood her face.

With the blunt honesty that sometimes got her into trouble, she muttered the only thing she could think of to say. "And I'd give more for you not to know."

She got up then, and hastily went back inside the motor home before he could say anything that would embarrass her further.

If that was possible, she thought ruefully.

She retreated to the bedroom and sat on the small, built-in settee that served as a chair, and in her case, too often a clothes basket. She wasn't surprised to realize she was trembling slightly.

She felt as if her world were spinning out of control. She was in danger, and because of that Marly was in danger, too. Yet she felt safe, protected, because of Draven. That she owed that feeling of shelter to the man who was connected to the worst nightmare of her life was an irony she didn't have the slightest idea how to deal with.

She had even less idea of how to deal with the fact she could no longer deny. She was attracted to him. Attracted in a way she'd thought herself long past, even before the damage to her body. Attracted in the way her pain and panic-racked body had responded in the first moment she'd looked up out of the rubble and seen him, in the way her mind had labeled him a harshly beautiful angel come to save her. Before the encounter had turned to torment.

She'd been truly surprised to find out Marly's guess had been right, and he'd expected her to hate him for what he'd had to do that day. And she'd meant every word she'd said, that she knew and believed he'd done what had to be done, and she was grateful. Grateful that she would see her daughter grow up, go to school, hopefully find her passion in life. Maybe marry someday, perhaps even have children of her own.

Grandchildren, Grace thought. Now there's a scary thought. You really are getting old if you're thinking about *that.*

But even that didn't bother her as much as it once had. Once she'd been confronted with the prospect of never growing old at all, the alternative seemed much more inviting.

She heard the phone in the other room ring. With an effort she reeled in her thoughts and stood up.

The ringing stopped. A moment later there was a tap on the door.

"Grace?"

Draven. She hadn't even heard him come in. But then, she'd already seen that he could move quieter than a cat.

"I heard it," she said as she opened the door. He was standing there with the cordless handset, which he now held out to her.

"It's Nick," he said.

She nodded and took it. "Yes, Nick," she said into the receiver.

"We'll be ready to start the first pour right after lunch."

She never missed this stage, and didn't want to start now. She looked at Draven. "I need to be there."

He nodded, and she told Nick she would be there in an hour. When she'd disconnected, Draven took the phone from her.

"You can do whatever you need to, go wherever you want now, as long as I'm with you. Buckley can handle Marly."

Her mouth quirked. "I'm sure he can."

She hadn't really realized what his calling in Kieren meant as far as her own freedom was concerned. That it was going to make it possible for her to resume her normal work habits.

At least, as normal as anything could get for her with John Draven glued to her.

The images that brought to mind threatened to send her scampering back to her bedroom until the blush faded again. Not that her bedroom was the best place to go to quash her rowdy thoughts.

"Lunch," she said abruptly. "I've got some Caribbean jerk chicken in the fridge. Sandwich?"

"You don't have to cook for me."

She knew he meant it; she wasn't sure what he did for meals, but he'd certainly never asked her.

"I said fridge. No cooking involved. For which," she added, "you should be grateful. My repertoire of edible food is limited, I'm afraid."

He gave her that half shrug she was starting to look at almost affectionately. "Nobody should be expected to build airports and cook, too."

She smiled at that, and decided to just fix the sandwiches. A few minutes later she had two rolls piled high with the local concoction of meat rubbed with spices, and "jerked" apart rather than cut into tidy slices. She'd grown to enjoy the particular blend that was available in Matola City, a recipe from Mr. Ayuso's mother.

That thought reminded her of Marly's escapade in the man's store, and something else she had wanted to say. She put the plates on the table, added a couple of glasses of lemonade and sat down, gesturing at Draven to join her. When he did, and had taken a bite, she spoke.

"I wanted to thank you."

"For what?" he asked after he'd swallowed.

"Everything. But right now, for Marly. Keeping her out of any further trouble."

The shrug again.

"I've been able to concentrate on my work better, not having to worry about her." She didn't mention the new distraction he himself was providing.

"Should be easier now, with Buckley."

She nodded. "Thanks for that, too. I appreciate the one-on-one for her."

He looked at her over the sandwich. "But not for you?"

She lowered her gaze to her own sandwich, still on the plate. "I didn't mean it that way."

"Having a bodyguard is tougher than being one."

She'd never thought about it that way. But then, she'd never really thought about it at all. At least, not in reference to herself.

"Anyway, thanks for bringing him."

Again the shrug. "I can't do the other part of my job and keep both of you safe, too."

"Find who's sabotaging us."

He nodded.

She hadn't thought of that. "I guess you haven't had much chance to work on that," she said.

"It's not at the top of the list."

She knew what Josh Redstone's priorities were. "Redstone people ever and always first," she quoted.

Draven nodded. "Doing what official or government agencies are supposed to handle comes in after all that, although Josh has no problem with us helping out if requested or needed. Of course, if somebody hurts one of his own, all bets are off."

Josh himself had told her that, when he'd first hired her. For the first time in a very long time, she'd felt part of a family, as if there were people she'd not even met yet who cared about her and would help if she needed them.

As Draven had. And still was.

"I meant what I said, about the earthquake," she said quietly. "I owe you my life."

"You owe me nothing."

"Same to you," she said.

His brows furrowed. "What?"

"You don't owe me anything. Most especially feeling haunted, whether it's ugly memories or horrible dreams."

He stared at her, for the first time since she'd known him an expression of surprise breaking through. She'd nailed it, she thought.

"They are ugly. And horrible," he said, surprising her in

turn with the admission. "And I don't know why. I've seen worse, done things like that a dozen times. But you…"

He trailed off, and she wondered what he'd been going to say. "I what?"

For a long moment she thought he wasn't going to answer. It was obvious he was battling, whether to speak or stop himself from speaking she didn't know.

"You were the worst," he finally said. "Having to hurt you."

"Why?"

This time the shrug annoyed her.

"You had to have done other things that made you feel that way," she said.

"Once." He stopped, and she waited, hoping her silence would work as it had before. Finally he continued. "When I had to tell Josh his big brother—and my closest friend—had died in my arms in the Gulf."

Grace blinked. This was a story she'd never heard. "Josh's brother?"

"We were on a recon mission. He was leading. Land mine."

The short, brusque words told her as much about his remembered pain as they did about what had happened. And his expression was odd, as if he couldn't quite believe he was talking about this.

Or perhaps, that he was talking about it to her.

"And that's how you met Josh?" she asked.

He nodded. "I tracked him down at the little airport Jim told me he hung out at. Told him. Stayed awhile, to make sure he was okay. Saw the way he was building Redstone. When I left the service, he offered me a job."

"And you've been with him ever since."

He nodded. Then, abruptly, he asked, "What about your own ugly memories and bad dreams?"

As a diversion, it was pretty blatant, but she let it pass. He'd already opened up more than she'd ever seen before.

"I still have them," she answered. "Fewer, farther between, but just as awful when they hit. I don't think you spend that long thinking you're going to die without it leaving some permanent scars."

"You don't. The fact that you're functioning at all is amazing."

"I don't feel amazing," she said frankly.

"You are," he said.

Grace fought down the sudden image that hit her, of him saying she was amazing in another context altogether. A very personal, intimate context.

At least one thing, she thought, *there wouldn't be any surprises. He knows exactly what happened to me, and what's missing.*

She gave herself a mental shake; thoughts like that were not going to help any. She grasped for something else, anything else, to talk about.

"Sometimes," she said, "I feel like I haven't really dealt with it at all. I fight so hard not to let the memories swamp me. Maybe I shouldn't."

"What do you think dealing with it is, except getting control over it?"

Lured by this unexpected openness, she asked, "Have you ever…felt that way? Swamped?"

He went very still.

"Sorry," she muttered. "That was a silly question. You're John Draven, you're always in control."

The sound that burst from him then was an oddly twisted combination of pained laughter and disgust.

"You know what I did, before I came here? I quit."

She drew back, staring at him. "You what?"

"I quit Redstone. I handed Josh my resignation."

John Draven quitting Redstone? That would be second only to St. John leaving, or even Josh himself.

"Why?" she asked, unable to stop herself.

He shook his head, clearly wishing he hadn't let it slip out.

"Why would you leave Josh?"

He swore under his breath. "He asked me the same thing. I didn't know...how that would feel for him to ask that."

"Why?" she asked again.

Again he didn't answer.

"There has to be a good reason. You wouldn't do it unless there was. You quit because...?"

"Because I can't trust myself anymore!"

The words burst from him as if on a torrent of pain, a rush of emotion she was certain he didn't often release. It seemed to suck all the oxygen out of the air, and she had to draw in a deep breath. He wasn't looking at her, in fact was obviously avoiding meeting her gaze, as if it would be too painful to look at another human being and see their reaction to that reluctant exclamation.

"Can't trust yourself?"

"I've lost it," he said, his tone almost bitter. "Fine thing to say to somebody I'm supposed to protect, but, damn it, it's true. Mr. Cool-and-Controlled can't hang on to his temper anymore."

Her forehead creased. "What do you mean?"

"Just what I said. My fuse isn't just short, it doesn't exist. The slightest thing sets me off."

"Everybody has days like that."

He grimaced. "Days I could handle. This has been months."

"Maybe you're just tired. If you usually go without sleep the way you have here, you can't help but be."

"When it interferes with the job, the reason for it doesn't matter."

She frowned. "But it hasn't interfered. You haven't lost your temper here."

"Barely," he muttered.

"Does that matter, as long as you haven't?" she asked, echoing his words back at him. "Besides, if you know you're on a short fuse, you'll be on guard about it. You're probably safer from losing it now than ever."

He stared at her, as if having trouble absorbing her words. She took advantage of his silence to rise and go wrap the second half of her sandwich; she'd made it far too large. And she wanted him to think about what she'd said; it was surprisingly painful to think of this solid, strong man of such legendary cool doubting himself.

She turned to go get her glass to wash, and literally collided with him. Again with that catlike silence, he'd gotten up to bring his plate and glass to the sink.

A little breathless, she reached for the dishes. At the same moment he leaned forward to set them on the counter. She sucked in her breath as they touched once again.

His hands went to her shoulders, as if to steady her, and she wondered if she was really as wobbly as she suddenly felt. And then his fingers tightened, hot and hard on her flesh.

"Grace," he said, his voice gone so low and rough it sent a shiver down her spine.

And then he kissed her.

Chapter 16

He should have known.

The alarms had gone off in his head even louder than the trip wires outside when he'd found himself telling this woman whatever she wanted to know. It had felt like a compulsion, one he didn't even know the source of but that he knew he couldn't ignore. And so it poured out, admissions, pain, feelings he rarely admitted he had to himself, let alone someone else.

Let alone to a woman, especially one he was attracted to. If you could call the fire and fury he was feeling mere attraction.

He'd done quite well at ignoring those alarms, however. Showing once more how out of control he really was. And if he hadn't been sure, the fire that surged in him the moment his lips touched hers would have seared the knowledge into his brain.

He hadn't meant to kiss her. It hadn't even been in his mind. Which was, perhaps, the problem. The urge had arisen out of some deep, primal need, and seemed to have bypassed his brain altogether. And the next thing he knew he was looking down into those incredible eyes of hers, and unable to stop himself.

It was all he could do to keep from ravaging her mouth. It had been so long, and she was sweeter than anything he'd ever tasted in his life. Warm and honey-rich, her lips softened beneath his, and if some part of his mind was startled that she didn't resist, he ignored that, too.

Not only could he not stop, he wanted more. He wanted it longer, hotter, deeper, and nearly shook with the effort to not overpower her and take what he needed so badly. But even as he thought it he realized *overpower* wasn't the word, that you didn't have to overpower someone who wasn't fighting back.

She wasn't fighting.

She wasn't fighting, or even protesting, in fact she was accepting, as if she wasn't surprised at all. Of course, why would a woman like Grace ever be surprised that any man was hungry to kiss her?

"Draven," she whispered against his mouth.

He drew back slightly. "All things considered," he said, "I think you should call me John."

And that in itself should have been a warning, but he ignored it. He reclaimed her mouth, and his hands slipped up to cup the back of her head, to steady her as he deepened the kiss. He felt a shiver of anticipation at the thought of exploring her thoroughly, endlessly. There wasn't a part of her he didn't want to—

The thump of feet on the outside steps sounded like an invasion in the suddenly heated silence. He felt Grace stiffen. With an effort as big as any he'd ever made in his life he did what he knew he had to. He tore his mouth away from those sweet, too-tempting lips.

A split second before the door swung open he made his unwilling hands follow suit and release her. They barely had time to separate before Marly marched in.

Thankfully she appeared too wrapped up in her own agenda to notice anything else. She spotted them in the kitchen, marched—there really was no other word for it— over to them and took a confrontational stance, her hands on her hips and her eyes heated.

When she spoke, her voice was just as angry as her gaze and body language. And it was directed at him.

"I don't need a babysitter, y'know, and I think it really sucks that you told Kieren I did."

They were apparently, he noted, already on a first name basis. That part of his plan had worked, at least. As to this part, this unexpected attack, he wasn't at all sure what to do. Which seemed to be a regular state of affairs for him when it came to Marly.

"It was just a phrase," he began, but she wasn't buying.

"Sure. He's just about the hottest guy I've ever seen, and you tell him to watch me like I'm some sort of child."

"I told him to watch you like you're possibly in danger," he retorted, "which is the truth."

"Babysitting," she insisted.

"Did he say something to make you feel that way?"

"Kieren? No, of course not. *He* would never make me feel like such a baby."

The inference that he would was unmistakable, and Draven smothered a sigh.

"We're going for a walk," Marly said, with an emphasis on the first word that made it clear she was already thinking of herself and Buckley as "we." "I'm going to show Kieren where everything is."

Without waiting for any assent or approval, she turned on her heel and marched out in much the same way as she'd marched in.

Draven watched the girl go, telling himself it was a good thing she'd come in when she had. He wasn't at all sure he could have stopped himself if she hadn't. But that she had, and the way she had, brought home to him once more that whatever he might feel, and even if Grace was willing to settle for what little he could give, he didn't think he could deal with Marly on a regular basis.

"Well, he's certainly charmed her," Grace said shakily.

"Yeah. It's me who can't deal with her."

"You did fine. You usually do with her. Besides, that wasn't really aimed at you, she was just embarrassed and striking out."

He shook his head. "I never know what to say to her."

Grace laughed. "You think I do? This whole parenting thing is a seat-of-the-pants kind of flying."

He shook his head again, more slowly. "I couldn't do it. Not every day, like you do. It would drive me crazy."

She went very quiet, the laugh vanishing, and taking the accompanying smile with it. He felt suddenly bereft, and wasn't quite sure what had happened.

"I understand," she said, her voice as cool as the change in her expression. "It's a rare man who's willing to take on a child that isn't his. I don't think the man willing to take on Marly at this difficult stage of life even exists."

Draven had no idea what he should say to a statement like that, so kept silent. Her expression changed subtly, as if from pain, or maybe resignation. And when she spoke again, her voice was brisk and businesslike.

"Now if you'll excuse me, I'm going to go change to go to the site."

She left him standing there, staring after her, troubled for reasons he didn't even begin to understand.

Two days later he was watching Grace watch the crew frame the walls of the small control tower building when his cell phone rang.

"Draven."

"Two possibles matching your partial plate registered with addresses on the island."

St. John's voice and clipped words were immediately recognizable.

"Go," he said.

"One. A Cecil Bedran. Registration expired several years ago. Check showed he's deceased."

"And number two?"

"More interesting. Current, but according to the record, it's on a 1972 Ford van."

"Hmm," Draven said. There was no way that car had been a van of any vintage. "Name?"

"Business name. Caribe Merchants. Post office box in Belize City."

When he heard the name, Draven's mind made the obvious leap instantaneously. He wondered if he was wrong about *el mercader*, if the drug dealer truly was behind the attacks and had been all along.

"Who are the primaries at Caribe?"

"Layered ownership. We're digging."

The moment he acknowledged the information St. John disconnected. Conversation with the man was always short, and sometimes painfully brief. He talked as if he had a finite number of words to use in his life, so he had to ration them.

"News?" Grace asked, coming up beside him.

"As much as you ever get out of St. John."

"Ah. So the saying's true?"

"What saying?"

"If Draven's a legend, St. John's a mystery."

Draven grimaced, but the expression faded as Grace's mouth curved upward. It was a natural enough smile, but he sensed the same uneasiness he'd felt in the past couple of days.

Ever since he'd kissed her.

"I've heard about him," she said. "Though I've never spoken to him for longer than a minute or two."

"I'm not sure that anybody except Josh ever has," he said dryly.

She smiled again, and again he felt the change in it. She was smiling at the comment, he thought, but wary of who had made it.

By necessity he had gotten fairly good over the years at reading people. And there was no doubt in his mind that Grace had changed. Or rather, her attitude toward him had changed. She was more watchful, more sensitive or more nervous, he wasn't sure which. Like she had been when he'd first arrived, yet different. In any case, it was putting him on edge, because he didn't know what to do about it.

That alone was unusual enough for Draven to bother him. In part it was because he wasn't used to not knowing what to do, but also because he didn't know if it was a continuation of the problem that had made him hand Josh his resignation, or if it was simply Grace herself who had derailed his usual mental acuity.

If he thought about that kiss, the answer to that question was clear.

If he thought about that kiss, the answer to anything else was lost in the heat.

"I need to head back to the trailer," she said. "I have to make some calls."

Unable to speak just then, he nodded, and they started to walk.

They needed to talk, he realized. Or do whatever it was going to take to get rid of this new tension between them.

The moment the thought formed in his head he recoiled inwardly. Was he actually thinking he *wanted* to initiate one of *those* kinds of talks with a woman? Had he gone totally crazy? Volunteering for something like that was way out of his comfort zone. He'd rather volunteer for armed combat.

Hell, those kinds of talks *were* armed combat, and the male of the species was usually weaponless.

"I guess I need to thank you again," Grace said.

Draven stopped in his tracks. Given his current thoughts, his mind shot to the impossible. He'd never been thanked for an unasked-for kiss before—not that there were many in the first place—and he doubted that record was about to be broken.

"Thank me for what?" he asked carefully as she stopped herself and turned to face him.

"Marly."

He let out a breath he hadn't even been aware of holding. "Marly?" he asked, his voice nearly normal now.

"That scene two days ago aside, she's...a different girl. Her old self, almost. But better."

He wasn't sure he didn't like the old Marly better, thorns and all. This new girl, all giggles and sweetness, didn't seem quite real to him. The old Marly had at least been honest. Blunt, angsty and occasionally rude, yes, but honest. He didn't quite trust any change that came about simply by the presence of a good-looking male.

Like you don't trust any change that comes about simply by the presence of a good-looking woman?

His own snide thought dug deep, stinging, and he spoke quickly, before she could ask what was wrong.

"Don't thank me, thank Buckley."

"But he's only here because you brought him."

He shrugged. "Needed another body. I remembered him from his interview."

"And you knew he'd charm Marly."

"Hoped."

"I just hope..." Her voice trailed off.

He stopped to look at her. "Hope what?"

She sighed. "That she doesn't get hurt."

"That was in his orders."

"What was?"

"Making sure Marly didn't get hurt."

Grace chuckled, but it was an odd, rueful sound. "You really don't know much about fourteen-year-old girls if you think that's within his control."

He wondered about the undertone, but he'd already admitted as much, and didn't see that there was anything more to add to her observation.

"He'll do what he can," he said instead.

They started to walk again, until this time Grace suddenly stopped.

"Darn," she said, in a disgusted tone. "I forgot some papers I need to call about the sealer delivery."

She started back. Draven turned to accompany her just as his cell rang again. This time the ID window said not St. John, but Buckley. He'd taken Marly out in the new inflatable an hour or so ago, so Draven let Grace get a little ahead of him before he answered in case Buckley had something to report that Grace shouldn't overhear. If something had happened to Marly, that wasn't the way he'd want her to find out.

"Draven," he answered finally, when Grace was out if immediate earshot.

"Buckley. We're just off the south tip of the island. Marly wants to go to Ambergris Cay, shopping or something. Thought I'd better run it by you first."

What was it with girls, women and shopping? he thought. He wondered if Grace had the same tendency. An image flashed through his mind, of trailing after her in some upscale mall. He should have recoiled at the very idea, but instead he found himself thinking about what watching her shop would tell him about her.

"Sir?"

Buckley's voice was uncertain, as if he thought the connection might have been dropped. Draven again dragged himself out of an uncharacteristic reverie. No matter what had happened between him and Grace, it was no excuse for losing focus.

Belatedly he considered Buckley's question for a moment. He knew Buckley would have had thorough training in all sorts of watercraft, it was part of Redstone's own, in-house academy of sorts. So that wasn't an issue; Marly would be safe with him running the boat, even in unfamiliar waters.

Besides, he knew that Buckley wasn't clearing it with him for that reason anyway; what he really wanted to know was if there was any reason connected to their situation here that they shouldn't go. Ambergris Cay to the south of them was the most developed island in the area, a tourist mecca, and as such was relatively safe. And his gut told him their problem was isolated, confined to this bit of land.

"Stay away from the north end here," he said. "And check in when you're back."

"Right."

"And make sure she pays for everything," he added. "We had a little acting-out problem a while back. Don't think it will recur, but keep on her."

"Yes, sir. Want me to call her mom?"

"No. I'll tell her."

He disconnected the call, and picked up his pace to catch up with Grace, who was just entering the structure that would eventually become the control tower above the small terminal building.

The building exploded into a fireball.

Chapter 17

It was a replay of her nightmare. With different special effects. Instead of the slow rumble of the earthquake that had built until it was impossible to stay on her feet, there was a single, huge flash and boom, knocking her off her feet in the first instant. Her ears were ringing, so much that she could barely hear the galelike rush of the firestorm.

She tried to move. Couldn't. Something was pinning her down. Something hard and heavy lay across her hips. The beam, she thought. The one that was supposed to hold up the terminal's roof. She pushed at it. It didn't move.

She almost screamed.

Just like before, she was trapped.

But this time she could burn alive before anyone got here.

So get yourself out, she ordered silently. She made herself focus, not think about Nick and the others, and who else might be trapped. Or worse. She could do nothing for them unless she got out herself.

She thought she heard a shout, but with her ears still ringing she couldn't be sure. She hoped so; it would mean at least someone else was alive. She looked around as best she could through eyes that were streaming tears in the midst of the smoke, to see what was within reach. Then she twisted, turned, trying to ignore the pain. By turning on her side she managed to raise the beam slightly with her own body. She stretched as far as she could and just managed to reach one of the cinder blocks that had been blown sideways out of the half-built wall. She pulled it toward her. With a tremendous effort she wedged it under the beam. When she rolled back, the pressure eased.

"Now or never," she muttered, and began to struggle to free herself from the still-tight fit.

For an agonizingly long moment, as the fire raced closer, gobbling up whatever fuel was in its path, she didn't think she was going to make it. And then, with a final shove using all her strength, she was free.

She heard the shout again. Her name. She scrambled to her knees, glanced at the inferno that was now a mere yard away.

"Over here!"

Her shout brought on a paroxysm of coughing. She decided to shut up and just get out while she could still breathe at all. But she could barely see, and the heat was getting so intense she was sure the fire was nearly at her. She knew she didn't have time to think about it. She simply had to take her best guess at which way to go and get moving.

She stayed on her knees and crawled. Wished she had something to tie over her nose and mouth to filter the smoke at least a little. She was beginning to feel disoriented. Wondered if she was going in circles. Then a strong hand grabbed her. She looked up through the swirling smoke. And once again the harsh angel was there, hovering, sheltering her, saving her.

"Can you stand?"

Reality snapped back into place. Draven. Of course. Who else would come marching through hell?

Her throat was so raw she didn't trust her voice to speak, so she answered him by standing. She expected him to lead her out, but instead she was suddenly airborne as he picked her up over his shoulder. She let out a yelp of surprise, but it instantly brought on the coughing fit she'd feared.

"Quiet," she heard him say.

Since she could barely breathe hanging upside down over his shoulder, she had little choice but to obey that order.

She closed her eyes against dizziness and the worsening sting of the smoke. The sensation of being upside down only furthered the disorientation she was feeling. She very much didn't want to pass out. She was afraid she'd never wake up again. She had cheated the reaper once before, she didn't know if she could get lucky twice.

She wasn't sure when it started, just became aware that the breath of air she'd just taken had been clean. Smokeless. Life-giving. Even as her somewhat sluggish brain recognized the fact she felt herself sliding to the ground. She tried to stand, but her knees seemed oddly wobbly. And then strong arms caught her under the shoulders and knees and lowered her gently. She opened her eyes and once more it was a flashback to that other nightmare day, only this time she knew the harsh angel, knew he was just a man. An incredibly strong, brave and haunted man.

And that made it seem even more of a miracle than it had been that day in Turkey.

"Are you all right?"

She wasn't sure. Her throat was viciously raw, her eyes bleary from smoke and tears, and she had to try to sense past that and assess the rest of her body.

She hurt here and there; she couldn't deny that. But when

she flexed muscles and bent joints everything seemed to work, with no sudden stabs of pain.

"I think so," she said, barely able to hear her own croak over the steady buzz. "I was trapped. Under a beam." She suppressed a shudder.

Draven said something she couldn't hear.

"Ears," she said.

"I'll bet," Draven said, his voice sounding rough, raspy, as if he'd breathed in as much smoke as she had. Or as if his throat were tight. "You were too damn close to the blast." He paused then, touching her cheek with surprising gentleness. "You saved yourself this time, Grace."

"But you—"

"I just helped you outside. You got yourself out of that trap, and that inferno."

The bigger picture snapped back into her mind. "Marly," she gasped.

"She's fine. Nowhere near the blast."

"Nick," she said, trying to get up. Draven gently but firmly stopped her.

"I saw him outside. He's all right."

"But the framing crew, and the others, they were—" She had to stop to cough, a heavy chest-straining cough.

"We'll find out in a minute," he said when the fit abated. "Look at me."

She did, only then realizing he was streaked with ash or soot just as she was, just not as thoroughly. He stared back into her eyes until she started to feel uncomfortable. Then he put one hand in front of her left eye.

"Keep them open," he instructed.

He was checking her pupils, she suddenly, belatedly realized. "I didn't hit my head," she said.

He didn't answer her. He moved his hand away quickly, then repeated the action with her other eye.

"I've had a concussion before—" she had to stop to cough again "—I know what it feels like. I don't have one."

"No, you don't."

Was he speaking louder than normal, she wondered, or were her ears clearing up? "Then can I get up?"

"No."

"I'm really fine," she said again.

"Just relax."

Only then did she realize he was methodically and gently running his hands over her.

"I don't think anything's broken," she said, her voice still rough.

"No," he agreed.

"Then what are you looking—"

"Blood," he said shortly.

"Oh."

"She all right?"

Although the ringing seemed to be lessening, she hadn't heard Nick approach. She looked up at him, glad to see he looked relatively unscathed.

"I'm fine," she said, feeling a little spurt of irritation when Nick looked to Draven for verification.

"Small burns. Nothing too bad. Probably some bad bruising to come."

"That," she said, "I can pretty well guarantee." She shifted her gaze back to Nick. "What about the crews?"

"They're all…accounted for."

She relaxed, letting out a sigh of relief. But then what he'd said and how he'd said it registered.

"What do you mean, 'accounted for'?"

"I'd say he means he knows where they are," Draven said. "Move your arm out this way. Then the other arm."

She flicked him a glance, wondering if he was trying to distract her. She looked back at Nick, her vision still blurry.

"Was anyone hurt?"

Nick hesitated. He glanced at Draven again, and tension spiked through her.

"You'll get a full report later, I'm sure," Draven said. "Right now we need to get you cleaned up."

Grace scrambled to her feet, catching Draven off guard enough to break free. She felt a little wobbly, but faced him as steadily as she could. She was still blinking rapidly, trying to clear her streaming eyes. She knew she must look frightening, but right now she didn't care.

"I'm responsible for this project, which means I'm responsible for the people on it," she said. She turned back to Nick. "Who's hurt? Do we need an airlift?"

"It's already on the way," Nick said.

In that moment her vision cleared, enough to see the look on his face.

"Oh, God," she whispered. "Who?"

Yet again Nick glanced at Draven. He had apparently become the man in charge, no matter what she said. And as the fire behind them began to finally ebb, she supposed she could see why. This was now his crime scene, or whatever Redstone Security called things like this.

After a quick glance at her, Draven finally nodded.

"Chuck." Nick's voice was tight. "And it's a lot worse."

Grace knew the two men had worked on several jobs together. And she also knew Chuck was one who had asked to be assigned to this job after he'd learned she was the project manager. She felt an aching sense of culpability; she'd never had a serious injury—other than her own—on a job before, not even the one struck by the earthquake. And now one man had been hurt twice.

Besides, she liked Chuck. He'd always been cheerful, worked hard and thought himself very lucky to be working for Redstone.

Nick's eyes were suspiciously bright, and he excused himself before, Grace guessed, he lost control. As he walked away, Grace felt the tiny shivers going through her. It must have been bad, for Nick to react this strongly. Would Chuck be the first death she'd ever had on a project?

She should have stayed on the ground, she thought through the fog of shock that enveloped her. Because right now she felt like she was going to fall down.

"Can you walk to the motor home, or shall I carry you?" Draven said.

She turned her head to look at him, and even that felt slow, as if she were trying to move underwater. "There are things I have to do. He has a wife, kids, they—"

"That will be handled."

"But if they need anything—"

"He and his family will have whatever is necessary, no matter what happens. Redstone takes care of its own."

"But I should call Debra—"

"Josh will call her."

She blinked at that. "Josh? Personally?"

"It's his policy. He is Redstone, and he feels he's ultimately responsible for everyone who works for him."

She felt both sadness at the circumstances, and pride in Redstone, Josh and everything they both stood for.

Draven repeated his original question.

"I can walk," she said. *I think,* she added silently.

She could, she found, but not well. The prosthetic foot seemed to have been twisted slightly, and was no longer properly seated on the stump. After a couple of limping steps she stopped to try to adjust it, although she suspected she was going to have to remove it and start over.

She never got the chance to try. The moment the problem became obvious, Draven literally swept her off her feet. It was the phrase that leapt to her mind; she couldn't help that, nor could she help the flood of color that rose to her cheeks as the other implications of the phrase echoed in her head.

"I can walk," she protested, but it sounded halfhearted even to her own ears.

"Quiet," he said as he settled her in his arms.

His voice sounded rough, and when she looked up at him she saw his jaw was set tightly. She knew his strength, had seen it evidenced, so she knew it wasn't a strain for him to carry her.

At least, not a physical one.

He carried her into the bathroom and gently let her down. Despite her efforts she wobbled. He moved quickly to brace her.

"I'm okay," she said.

He ignored her, and began to peel off her filthy clothes. Startled, she pulled back.

"Just be still," he said, his voice as tight as his jaw had been. There was an undertone in it she didn't recognize, because she'd never heard it before.

She felt herself coloring hotly as he continued, but still noted how gently he touched her, how carefully he pulled her filthy, smoke-and-ash saturated clothes off. She shivered when she was left in nothing but her underwear, but she wasn't at all cold. Embarrassed at the plain, cotton, utilitarian undergarments, perhaps, but nothing fancier was comfortable or practical on a job, especially in this climate.

Odd, she thought with a sort of distant vagueness, that she wasn't at all embarrassed about her foot. How could she be, when this was the man who knew better than anyone but her doctors what she'd been left to deal with?

And then he unhooked her bra, with a slight awkwardness that somehow reassured her. She felt the motion of her breasts as they were freed, and an unusual little sting from a spot on the left one. She looked and saw a reddened spot where an ember or something had given her a small burn.

Even as she looked, she saw Draven's hand move. She sucked in a breath as his strong, tough hand cupped the soft flesh and lifted. She felt an odd tremor through his hands, as if he were trembling. And that reassured her even more. She didn't pull away, couldn't, as a memory of her dream flashed through her head. Instead she barely quashed the urge to push forward, pressing herself into his palm.

Slowly, so slowly she nearly cried out with anticipation, he bent his head and kissed that spot, so gently she felt only the barest brush of his lips.

She wobbled again, but for a completely different reason this time. She felt a shiver go through her, followed by a rush of heat that seemed to pool low and deep. Draven must have felt it, too, because he raised his head and looked at her, his eyes hot with something she had never expected to see in those cool, green depths. Except in dreams…

He began to move quickly then, stripping off her panties and then, after a moment's study, removing the prosthesis as if he did it every day. Again oddly, she didn't feel awkward at being naked in front of him—in fact, judging from that building heat, she instead found it arousing—but only wondered if she was going to be able to hop into the shower.

And then Draven solved the problem by lifting her in his arms and stepping into the shower himself.

"You're going to get wet," she protested.

"Don't worry about it."

"But you're dressed."

"That," he said gruffly, "could be fixed, but I'm not sure you'd like the results."

Again her breath caught as she realized what he was saying. And stopped entirely when she realized that she wanted it. More than she could ever remember wanting anything in her life.

"*I'm* sure," she said.

He went rigidly still. "What?"

"I'm sure I'll like it."

"Grace—"

He stopped as she reached up to cup his cheek. Slowly he let her slip down to the tile. She held on to him for balance…and because she wanted to. He stared down at her.

"Don't, Grace. Don't start if you don't mean to finish."

"I won't," she said. "I mean it."

And then she reached for his hand. Slowly she drew it upward, until it was once more cupping her breast.

She heard him suck in a breath. And then, almost convulsively, his fingers curved around her.

As if making a final effort at warning he said thickly, "Don't count on me to stop unless we do it now. I've wanted this for too long."

Me, too, she thought, unable to speak it with his hand on her. So in answer she balanced against the wall of the shower, took his other hand and urged it toward her other breast.

Draven groaned aloud. Grace felt the rumble deep in his chest before she heard the sound. She pressed closer and felt the surge of male hardness against her. Then she felt a shudder go through him, and the knowledge of his response only stoked the fire building inside her.

And then he began to move. Quickly. Making sure she was safely balanced, he backed up a step and yanked off his own clothes. She looked at his hard, leanly muscled body, at the sleek skin and the scars that marked it. Looked at the broad chest; the lean, flat belly; and below to the thick curls surrounding jutting, rigid flesh. A shiver went through her at the thought of it buried inside her, and the heat within became almost unbearable.

He reached past her and turned the tap. The water turned warm almost immediately, thanks to the proximity of the motor home's water heater. Draven grabbed the soap, but ignored the washcloth on the rack. When she realized why she shivered again; he was going to wash her himself, with his bare hands.

She nearly moaned as he began, his soap-slick hands sliding over her. And then he cupped her breasts again, and slid his thumbs over peaks already taut, and she did moan. He made a deep, guttural sound in response. Then he caught her taut nipples between his fingers and gently squeezed and flicked them until she cried out at the intensity of the sensation.

She thought for a moment she was going to fall, but he steadied her even as his hands slid down her body, rubbing gently, soaping and rinsing in turn. When he reached her legs, she felt the first flicker of apprehension, but he bathed her stump as tenderly as the rest of her, adding a bit of gentle massage that felt wonderful.

He worked his way back up, slowly, so slowly that she was in an agony of anticipation by the time his slick hands slid between her thighs. She knew the fierceness of her own arousal by the ease and speed with which he found the swollen knot of nerves that were already aching for his touch. He circled, caressed and stroked until she knew she was going to explode if he didn't stop.

"Please, John," she begged, not sure what she was begging for.

"Johnny seems right now," he said, and through the haze she was vaguely aware he looked somewhat surprised at his own words.

"Johnny," she whispered, trying it, liking this name that she would never have dared use on her own.

"Relax," he said. "Just let go."

"But—"

He kissed her then, swamping her protest in a wave of

heat so searing she lost all awareness of anything except his lips taking her mouth and his hands claiming her body. She knew her own slick readiness by the way his finger slid into her. Knew how close she was by the sensation of her body clenching around the invasion.

He broke the kiss and swore under his breath as she tightened. She could feel his body tense.

"Not without you," she choked out. "Please."

He shuddered, as if fighting something, and then began again. He stroked her, rubbing that now violently aroused knot of nerve endings. And then he lowered his head and caught one stiff nipple in his mouth and sucked deeply.

Grace heard herself cry out as her body rippled with wave after wave of fiery sensation. And still he kept on, driving her higher, until she was shaking with the force of it.

And then, in one smooth motion, he lifted her, pulled her legs around him and stepped out of the shower. He took her down to the floor with exquisite care. He came down with her and into her in the same movement, driving himself hard and deep, filling and stretching her to the edge of unbearable sensation.

Grace screamed at the hard, driving, huge invasion of flesh into a body already on the edge. And then he moved again, pulling back and driving home again, and she shattered. Some small part of her mind knew she was wild with it; she felt herself buck and twist like some wild thing impaled by incredible pleasure. She grabbed at him, clutched at him, at any part of him she could reach to grind closer, take him deeper.

When he groaned her name as his body surged into her one last time, when she felt him shudder beneath her hands and explode inside her, when he held on to her as if she were the only thing left in his world, Grace thought there was nothing more to be asked of this life.

* * *

Draven woke up, amazed that he'd slept in the middle of the day. Even as tired as he was, that was unusual. And instead of his usual instant alertness, he came back to awareness slowly, in a drifting sort of way he'd never experienced before.

But he'd never experienced anything like what had happened here, either. From the shower to the bathroom floor to Grace's bed, he'd been like some crazed man, starved for something he'd never known existed. Because he'd never known anything like the incredible sensation of sinking into her and feeling as if he'd found home at last, or like the hot, swift passion that had swept them both upward to explode in a firestorm rivaling the one that had nearly separated them forever.

He shied away from the implications of that as he gradually became more awake. He would sort that out later, he thought as he fought off the last groggy remnants of the unaccustomed afternoon sleep. Right now, he had other things to think about. Other things to do.

But one thing was crystal clear to him now, as he lay there holding this gallant, lovely, unexpectedly sensual woman in his arms. He was tired of just reacting. Tired of guarding against instead of solving the problem. *El mercader* had given him the information he needed.

It was time to go on the offensive.

Chapter 18

Grace awoke in the early twilight, feeling oddly energized after her two-hour nap. She would have expected to still feel shaken by the explosion, but with the exception of the expected aches, she felt good.

And some unexpected aches.

The memories flooded back, reminding her of exactly why she felt so energized. For a moment she just lay there as the erotic heat swept over her anew, as if he were still touching her, still caressing her.

As if he were still here.

She jolted upright. Stared at the empty space in the bed next to her. Felt an answering emptiness building inside her. Had he simply gone? Without a word? Gotten what he wanted and casually left her to wake up feeling alone and lost?

Was she suddenly drowning in cliché?

She said it to herself sarcastically as common sense

flooded back in. Everything she knew about John Draven told her he didn't take anything lightly. Just because she was a little emotionally scarred didn't mean she should assume this was any different. Long ago, after realizing her imaginings were so often worse than the reality came to be, she'd sworn not to spend any of her life going to meet a ship full of troubles that hadn't docked yet.

Calmer now, she stretched, wincing when a sore spot protested. Bruises hadn't shown up yet, but she knew they would soon.

She heard a sound from the other room. And chided herself for the way her pulse sped up at the realization that he hadn't left after all.

She got up, pondered what she should do about dressing. After the afternoon they'd spent, naked on her bed and exploring each other in the tropical light, worrying about covering up seemed a bit absurd. But it was still too new, too fragile, so she got out a full set of clean clothes.

She reached for the prosthetic foot, which had gotten fairly grubby amid the smoke and ashes. To her surprise it was clean. She didn't think she was that fuzzy that'd she'd tidied it up and didn't remember, and Marly wouldn't have done it even if she'd been back from her trip to Ambergris.

Which left Draven. John. Johnny, she said to herself, and it made her shiver to remember when he'd told her to use the name she instinctively knew few were given permission to use.

The thought that he had cleaned the prosthesis for her made her feel a tightness in her throat. She couldn't remember anyone doing something like that for her, only to help, without being asked and without expecting anything in return. And he'd clearly felt no qualms, just as his only reaction to the sight of her stump had been to kiss the scars as

the beginning of a sensual foray that had ended with her stifling a scream she was sure would have been heard in
Belize City.

She powdered, put on a fresh stump sock and the foot,
then dressed quickly. She quietly opened the door and
stepped into the main room of the motor home.

And stopped dead.

She knew the man in front of her had to be Draven, but
it was a Draven she'd never seen before. It wasn't simply that
he was dressed in different clothes—black jeans and shirt
and a loose jacket—or that he had his hair dampened and
slicked back, giving him an even more ascetic look.

It was his face. His expression. Always severe, now it
was hard-edged, unyielding, bordering on fierce. And it
was the way he was moving. He always had a tight-knit
sort of grace about him, but now he was moving as if he
barely had a leash on some building storm inside him. She
could sense an imminent detonation, and she had the sudden thought that when John Draven exploded, it was entirely possible that he could do more damage than the pipe
bomb he'd told her had blown up the half-finished terminal building.

When she saw what he was doing, her heart slammed into
her throat.

He was arming himself. Not just the automatic weapon
she'd seen before at the small of his back, but also another,
smaller one in a holster strapped to his ankle.

Then he picked a knife up from the sofa and slipped it into
his boot. A military-style knife that looked painfully like the
one he'd used on her, that day that now seemed so long ago.
But it hadn't been this Draven who had done that. This was
no harsh angel; this was a warrior. A warrior who wouldn't
be stopped by anything short of death.

He picked up something else that looked like a coiled cord

and put it in his left jacket pocket. Something else she didn't recognize, a small case of some kind, went in the other jacket pocket.

He turned then. She thought he hadn't been aware of her presence, but the minute he faced her she knew he'd known all along she was standing there. She felt a shiver go down her spine as a being she'd never seen before looked back at her. The first word that popped into her head was frightening.

Predator.

She swallowed tightly against the sudden dryness of her mouth. She opened her mouth to speak, could think of nothing to say and closed it again.

When he spoke, his voice was a chilly, emotionless thing that matched the expression on his face and the flat, almost bleak look in his eyes.

"I've called Buckley. They're almost back here. He'll take over."

He picked up something else from the sofa and held it out to her. She barely glanced at it before she took it, feeling mesmerized by the changes in him.

"That's a private satellite phone. Dial five-five and you'll have a direct, scrambled connection to Redstone headquarters."

She finally managed to find her voice. "Why do I need that?"

"If anything else happens here, tell Buckley. If something happens to him, you use that."

She looked down at the device, which looked like a slightly oversize cell phone. She stared at it, not wanting to ask the obvious question of why he was giving it to her.

"But you said to call you," she managed to get out.

"I'll be out of touch until I get back."

"Back." She said it flatly as he confirmed her guess. He

was leaving. Leaving to do…something she didn't even want to think about. And before she could stop herself the question came out. "And if you don't come back?"

He didn't even blink. "Buckley will take over."

Just like that. As if this was routine. As if walking into danger that could possibly prove fatal was something he did so often it didn't merit acknowledgment.

And as soon as she thought it, she realized it was quite possibly true.

"What are you going to do—"

The opening of the outer door interrupted the question she didn't really want answered. Marly and her shadow came in, the girl chattering excitedly, Buckley making a very creditable pretense of interest.

Then Marly saw Draven. Even the teenager saw the change. Grace wondered if this was how she had looked when she'd first seen him like this, with that sort of stunned, uneasy expression on her face.

Only Buckley didn't react. Grace wondered if that was because he'd seen this Draven before, or if it was because he could undergo the same kind of change himself. She tried to imagine the golden boy as something dark and dangerous. The image just wouldn't form.

She understood that she was focusing on Buckley to avoid dealing with Draven's transformation. To have the man she had spent the most incredible hours of her life with go from lover to…whatever he'd become was more than she could handle right now.

She told herself she shouldn't be surprised. Hadn't he gone from a gentle, careful and unhurried lover to a fierce, rough and demanding one in the space of an afternoon? That she had reveled in both was something else she couldn't deal with at the moment, in the face of this conversion.

"What are you doing?" Marly asked him, her voice tiny.

"Ending this," he said, and Marly reacted to the changed voice just as Grace had, drawing back slightly.

At last Grace regained her voice, although she guessed it sounded much like her daughter's had. "Where are you going?"

Draven looked at her then. She thought she saw a brief flicker of something warmer in that icy gaze, but it was gone so swiftly she couldn't be sure. But his next word, short and deadly, blasted the thought out of her mind.

"Hunting."

It was a few minutes after Draven was gone that, as if he felt he should say something, Buckley spoke.

"He really is the best."

"I'm sure he is," Grace muttered.

"Don't worry about him. He may be hunting a bad guy, but I'd back Mr. Draven against any five men you could come up with."

She didn't like the fact that her state of mind had become so obvious. And she certainly didn't want what had happened between them to become known until she'd had a chance to work through her roiling emotions.

Especially in front of her too-young, impressionable daughter.

"I'm not worried," she said.

How big a lie that was she wasn't certain. She knew his reputation, and now that she'd seen him in hunting mode, she had to believe it was well earned. But he had given her that phone. To use if he didn't come back.

To use if he was killed.

She fought back the shiver that threatened to ripple through her. She told herself she really shouldn't worry. He knew what he was doing. Hadn't his metamorphosis from lover to predator shocked her into speechlessness?

"He looked…scary," Marly said, still in that tiny voice. "I've never seen him look like that."

"It's part of why he's so good at what he does," Buckley said to the girl. "The people he goes up against see just what you did. And they think twice. Some of them just give up without a fight, after seeing that look."

All Grace could think about was what it had taken in his life to put that look in his eyes.

She'd never felt so tangled up inside. Her memories of this afternoon were colliding with the man she'd seen leave here. She wasn't sure if the two could ever be reconciled. Wasn't even sure she wanted to reconcile them.

But how would she feel if he didn't come back? If something went fatally wrong?

Her mind shied away from that. She told herself he wouldn't be chief of Redstone Security if he made mistakes. That he was capable of handling anything that came along. He was capable of taking care of himself. Capable of resolving any situation. John Draven could handle anything.

While she didn't know if she was capable of handling the simple fact that, fool that she was, she might be in love with him.

Draven tossed the coiled metal line over the ten-foot wood barricade, tugged until the hook on the end grabbed and held. Hand over hand he walked up the wall, then gripped the top and pulled himself up. He checked the other side, picked a spot just big enough behind a hibiscus covered with pink blooms, and went over. He landed with little more than a faint thud, and continued down into a crouch behind the shrub in one smooth movement.

He waited, listening. He'd watched the compound from the roof of an abandoned building a quarter mile away, using one of Redstone Technology's latest compact spotting scopes. The house and three outbuildings—one of them probably a meth lab or something, he guessed—stood just where the island started to narrow toward the point at the north end. The sandbar that extended out from the point curved toward the mainland and disappeared into the turquoise water a couple of hundred yards out.

He'd observed for a couple of hours, noting that there didn't appear to be any guard dogs, and timing the intervals at which he saw any movement of people outside and along the tall wooden barricade that had been built around the five or so acres surrounding the sprawling two-story house.

His next step had been to switch on the infrared feature on the scope, to look for signs of an alarm system. Nothing registered. When he got close enough, he did a physical inspection, again looking for any sign of an alarm. He still found nothing. So either they had something so new he didn't know about it yet, or they weren't worried. Without arrogance, he guessed it was the latter; Redstone usually came up with the cutting-edge stuff, and he was one of the first to know about it.

He timed his arrival at the spot he'd chosen at an unpatrolled moment. He crouched and waited. Saw and heard nothing.

He began to work his way toward the house. Some effort had been made to keep the area clear of undergrowth, but in this tropical place it was a full-time job to just stay even. He was thankful for that, because it offered enough cover for him to make it to the edge of the ornately landscaped area around the glistening pool without being spotted. After that, it didn't matter.

He emerged from the still-wild area into the formal part of the yard, designed by, in his view, somebody with too much money and too little taste. But he had learned early on that it was wise to learn as much as possible about your adversary, and what they chose to live with was information that contributed to that goal. So he studied the garden anyway.

Ornate statuary was everywhere, including several religious icons he found more than a little ironic given that they were gracing the property of a drug dealer. He strolled past a gilded statue of a pudgy cherub with a bow and some tiny arrows that he supposed was supposed to be Cupid, which stood a few feet away from a Madonna that was even more ornate.

Irony, he thought, wasn't a strong enough word.

He reached the flagstone deck around the lagoon-style pool. Drugs still paid well, obviously. He glanced at the house, and the tall, spacious windows on the wall facing away from the coast of Belize and looking at the open sea.

Off to one side, parked on a gravel area, he saw several vehicles, most of them showing the wear and tear of the tropical climate. The fancy wheels he assumed were around must be safely tucked in the large garage he could just see the corner of.

As he went a little farther, he was able to see the last car in the row. He stopped, staring at it. Checked the license plate.

It was the car he'd seen speeding away from the construction site. And the license was not the one registered to Caribe Merchants, but rather the one St. John had told him came back registered to a deceased man.

Had his gut been wrong? Had it truly been *el mercader* all along?

His brain, already in high gear, processed the idea quickly, and he realized it didn't make any difference, he would still be here, handling it the same way.

He stepped out onto the patio and considered the deck furniture that was nearly as elaborate as the statuary had been, chose the least obnoxious lounge of the group. He sat on the edge, glad it was less uncomfortable than it looked.

He swung around to stretch out on the lounge, crossing his feet casually at the ankles.

He relaxed and waited for *el mercader* to notice he was here.

Chapter 19

When the guards finally spotted him, they were so startled that it clearly took them a moment to believe what they were seeing. Draven had interlaced his fingers behind his head as he relaxed on the lounge, making it clear he had no plans to reach for any weapon he might have. It was a gamble, but he was counting on curiosity to keep him alive.

The first thing the men did was draw down on him. That told him their boss didn't believe in taking chances. The fact that they didn't shoot him on sight told him *el mercader* didn't believe in shooting first and asking questions later. It wasn't much, but it was enough to start with.

One of the men spoke into a two-way radio while the other did a perfunctory pat-down search. He found the weapon at the small of Draven's back. Draven didn't wince even inwardly. The two-inch .38 was still strapped to his leg and the Ka-bar knife with the high-carbon, seven-inch blade was still tucked into his boot.

But he also noticed the faintest tinge of purple on the man's hands. Between the presence of the car and the remnants of the dye, he knew this was the man who'd tripped the alarm.

He was escorted rather forcefully into the house. And there he got his second surprise. He'd expected the interior of the house to reflect the same gaudy taste as the outside, but instead it had a completely different feel. The décor was expensive, light colors that emphasized the balminess of the climate and sturdy pieces of furniture that anchored the whole without weighing it down, a classic island effect.

Classic, and classier, was his first thought. The juxtaposition of the outside and inside was startling. And as he was escorted through the house, he wasn't sure what this difference added to his assessment of *el mercader.*

They shoved him into a room that for all the world looked like an English library, complete with dark green walls and floor-to-ceiling bookcases. They tossed the Glock onto the huge, cherrywood desk, in front of the man who sat in the leather executive-type chair. And Draven had to reassess yet again.

He knew what the average person's image of a Central American drug dealer was. Slick, dripping in gold jewelry, dressed in expensive clothes, whatever the stereotype was, *el mercader* didn't fit it. He didn't fit the tacky display outside, either.

Nor, Draven had realized with the first words out of the man's mouth, was he Central American. Draven got most of what he spat out angrily to the two guards, chewing them out for letting him get so far, because it was said in that Americanized combination of Spanish and English known as Spanglish, used mostly by people who had grown up speaking both. And if the near-blond color of his hair was any indicator, his heritage was at least partly on the English-speaking side.

The two men left hastily the moment their boss released them. Draven took a seat in a chair opposite the desk without being asked, and noted that while the man's eyebrows lifted slightly, he said nothing.

"So," Draven said as if he were visiting the new home of a friend, "when did you change decorators?"

The brows lowered as *el mercader* blinked. "What?"

"Inside. Did it used to look like the outside?"

The man drew back slightly. His expression was an odd one, hard to interpret, but Draven thought he saw the faintest twitch at one corner of his mouth, as if he were trying not to smile or chuckle.

"Yes," the man said. "But it left with the woman who produced it. My ex-wife is off to turn some other man's home into a nightmare."

It was, as he'd guessed, the voice of a native English speaker. And a well-spoken one at that.

"Good choice," Draven said, and again saw the mouth twitch. But any trace of amusement vanished as the man leaned back in his chair, looking across at Draven.

"You better have a good reason for being here, *pendejo*."

Draven ignored the last insulting word, thinking instead that it was interesting that the first question wasn't "Who are you?" There was only one reasonable assumption to make, and that was that the man already knew who he was.

"I think so," Draven said mildly.

He waited, letting the silence spin out. He held the man's gaze steadily, knowing it was becoming a contest of who would break first. And knowing it wouldn't be him; he'd done this too many times, with men tougher than this one, men who could afford but wouldn't allow themselves this kind of luxury, for fear it would soften them.

El mercader broke.

"You are Redstone," he said, in the tone of someone expecting to surprise his listener. Since he'd already deduced the man knew who he was, Draven was easily able to keep any flicker of expression off his face, and out of his voice.

"And you are *el mercader.*"

This time the twitch broke through to a grin. "Now that we have that clear, I repeat, why are you here?"

"To find out who is hiding behind the nickname."

The grin vanished. *El mercader* tensed, and Draven made ready to move quickly if he had to. But he continued speaking, as if he'd noticed nothing.

"And to learn if he is the one I have to stop."

The man's expression went from antagonism to curiosity in the space of a moment. "Most," he said, "have already decided that."

So, as Draven had figured, he knew that he was the prime suspect. "I'm not convinced," he said.

The man leaned forward, looking at Draven intently. "Why?"

"Because you're the most obvious."

"Sometimes the obvious is the truth."

"Sometimes," Draven agreed.

"What makes you think that is not true this time?"

"Thinking has nothing to do with it."

"Ah. I appreciate a man who trusts his instincts." *El mercader* leaned back in his chair, smiling now. "No, I am not the one you need to stop."

Draven believed him. There was always the chance he was misjudging, and he wasn't one hundred per cent confident in what his gut was telling him these days, but he had little choice but to trust it once again.

"If that's the case, then perhaps I should tell you your men need a little more practice. Or perhaps a little more… motivation."

The man behind the desk frowned. "What do you mean?"

Draven held up his hands, palm out, to show his peaceful intent. Then he lifted one foot to his other knee and pulled out his knife and set it on the edge of the desk. *El mercader* swore, loudly.

But when Draven switched feet and pulled out the small, .38 revolver, the man leapt to his feet. Draven's Spanish was better than adequate, but even he couldn't follow the string of furious words that followed. After another moment *el mercader* sat back down. Draven didn't envy the two men who were going to bear the brunt of their boss's wrath.

But the action had done what he hoped, removed the man's last doubts about his sincerity at this moment. After a moment spent calming down, the man returned to the matter at hand. He continued as if nothing had happened. So he could, Draven noted, compartmentalize, even when angry. A good sign for what he was here to propose.

"I have no interest in your little airstrip," *el mercader* said. "I do no business here."

"So I've heard."

"It is a smart man who keeps his home clean."

"And it is a smart man in your business whose real name is still unknown."

A small smile returned at the acknowledgment, or perhaps at the admission that Draven had tried and failed to learn who he was.

"My secret is satisfaction," *el mercader* said. "I am happy where I am, with my little corner. I protect what I have, but I don't need to expand. I don't trespass on anyone else's turf."

"A smart man," Draven repeated, continuing to play to the man's obviously strong ego. He'd do what he had to to put an end to this. "Smart enough to see a good deal when it's offered."

The man looked startled, then amused, and finally interested. "What kind of deal would Redstone possibly want to make with me? I find it hard to believe they are interested in my business."

"Not yet," Draven said.

One brow shot upward. "I see."

Draven suspected that he did. He himself knew that eventually, when Redstone began operations, he'd have to take the man down. Cleaning up such problems was another side benefit of having Redstone come to your part of the world. They only got involved if it impacted Redstone directly, but if they did, the problem was inevitably solved.

Draven leaned back in his own chair, rested his elbows on the plush arms and steepled his fingers in front of him. "How has life been lately?"

That twist of the lips again. "Annoying," *el mercader* said. "The esteemed Sergeant Espinoza harassing my people, Mayor Remington writing editorials accusing me, myself being followed whenever I leave the grounds."

"Very annoying," Draven agreed.

"I am tired of taking the blame for your troubles. There is enough I am guilty of, without taking the rap for things I haven't done."

Draven nodded. He'd been hoping for just that mindset.

"Then I will tell you that your immediate future can be improved."

The man looked thoughtful. Draven doubted he'd missed the implication that his long-term future was another matter, but he'd obviously decided that was to be dealt with when the time came.

"You know the locals. Do you have any suspicions on who might be involved?" Draven asked.

"I have some ideas, yes. You have a plan?"

"Yes."

The man behind the desk studied him intently once more. Draven stayed silent, knowing it was now in his court.

"Talk," *el mercader* finally said.

Draven talked.

Grace finally stopped pacing, only because the bruises were beginning to make themselves felt. When she started to limp because her hip was aching where the beam had come down on her, she finally sat down.

"Are you all right?"

Marly's voice was more concerned than Grace could recall in recent memory. When Nick had come to the motor home to check on Grace, he had inadvertently let out more details of the explosion than Grace would have told her daughter, especially about how close she had come to being killed. The girl had been a bit clingy ever since.

It was the opposite of how she'd been after the earthquake, when she'd seemed to pull away and to want little to do with her mother or even acknowledge what had happened. Grace wondered what had caused the change, but welcomed it. She hoped it wasn't just a temporary mood, as Marly's so often seemed to be these days.

"Just a little stiff," she answered.

"Can I get you anything?"

That offer was so uncharacteristic of the girl of late that Grace couldn't help staring at her. Marly flushed, as if she knew exactly what her mother was thinking.

"No," Grace said, "but, thank you. Very much."

She hoped the girl realized she meant for more than the simple offer. She thought perhaps she did when Marly looked up and gave her a small smile.

Later, when Marly and Kieren were involved in a video game as if they were both of an age, Grace found herself doing exactly what she'd sworn not to: sitting by the window waiting for Draven to return. And no amount of chiding herself for being an idiotic, moonstruck female helped.

But then, the average idiotic, moonstruck female wasn't waiting for a man who might not make it back alive.

After another hour, when Marly and Kieren had given up on the video game, Grace stood up. She winced once more as her body protested.

"Mom?"

Grace made a quick decision. "Would you go in the bathroom and find the aspirin for me?"

"Sure."

The girl hurried off to the bathroom. Grace turned to Kieren. "Where did he go?"

The young man gave her a startled look. She realized she'd used the tone she used to give orders on a job. But at this point she didn't care, she just wanted an answer.

"I don't know," Kieren said. Grace stared him down. "I mean it," he said after a moment. "All he told me was that this was going to end, now, and not to let either one of you out of my sight."

"And to call Redstone if he didn't come back?"

"Well, yeah, of course, but—"

He broke off as she turned away and headed for the door.

"Ms. O'Conner," he said, leaping to his feet.

She kept going. Reached for the door handle. Before she could grasp it, Kieren was there, slipping between her and the door.

"I can't let you go out," he said. "Mr. Draven's orders."

"I'm going," she said. "Your job is to keep my daughter safe."

"Both of you," he said.

"I'm releasing you from that."

"I'm very sorry Ms. O'Conner, but you can't do that. I answer to Mr. Draven."

"But he's not here."

"Doesn't matter. He'll expect me to carry his orders out, no matter what. I'm supposed to keep both of you here."

"Then you've got a problem."

Kieren said gently, "No, Ms. O'Conner, I'm afraid you do."

"You'll have to physically stop me."

Kieren sighed and said, "Then that's what I'll do. Reluctantly, but I will do it."

"I'm sure Mr. Draven wouldn't like it if you hurt the person you're guarding."

"No, he wouldn't. That's why he makes sure we're trained so well nobody gets hurt. But I'd be a lot happier if I didn't have to worry about it," he said.

"Mom?" Marly's voice came, somewhat muffled, from the bathroom. "I can't find the aspirin."

Grace, who had known perfectly well they weren't in there but had needed Marly out of the room for a moment, called back to her, "Try the bedroom, then. I think it may be in a drawer. Thanks, honey."

Grace, who had never taken her eyes off Kieren, continued to study him for a long silent moment. He returned her gaze levelly, never dodging, never blinking. A solid, steadfast core became evident, and in that moment she revised her earlier opinion. Suddenly she could picture him transforming as Draven had, into something powerful and dangerous.

"And if I asked you if you'd really fight a woman, and a disabled one at that?"

It was his turn to study her. And then, softly, he said, "I'd wonder if you were really the woman Mr. Draven told me about. She would never trade on her physical condition."

Kieren Buckley, it seemed, was indeed dangerous, and in more ways than one.

"I believe we have an impasse," she said.

"No, ma'am. I believe I've won."

"Presumptuous of you."

"No, Ms. O'Conner. It's just that Draven is never wrong about people. And there's no way you'd do something that would get me fired."

She gave him a sideways look, and despite her emotional state, he looked so innocently solemn she couldn't help but smile.

"You are good, aren't you?" she said. "Does Redstone have a class in Manipulation 101?"

"Yes, ma'am," he said with a grin. "Although it's got a much fancier name."

"I'm sure it does. Does your boss teach it?"

Kieren laughed. "No. He brought in a psychologist, a guy who served with him in the rangers."

The memory of what Draven had told her about Josh's brother flashed through her mind, and she wondered if Draven had seen that psychologist afterward. Her image of how he must have been back then didn't really fit with that idea. She'd always thought men like army rangers, whose motto, she'd learned, was "Rangers lead the way" because they were the first into any dangerous situation, would think themselves too macho for that kind of help. But perhaps even the army had seen the necessity. Or perhaps she'd just had the wrong idea all along.

"Got it!" Marly said as she came back into the room, carrying the small bottle. "It was in the top dresser drawer, with your leg powder."

She stopped, looking at the two of them, still standing beside the door. Suspicion crossed her face.

"Thanks," Grace said again, hoping to divert her.

"Yeah. What's going on?"

So much for that idea, Grace thought. "We were just talking," she said, giving Kieren a warning glance.

"About Redstone Security training," the young man put in.

Marly looked from one to the other, clearly doubtful.

"I'm thinking of sending you," Grace said in an effort at a diverting joke.

Marly's eyes widened. "Wow, that would be cool!"

Not the response she was expecting, Grace thought ruefully. But as a distraction it had worked. She would probably regret the joke, but—

The door swung open. All three occupants of the motor home spun around.

Draven was back.

Grace couldn't stop herself from looking him up and down. At first she was looking for any sign of injury. But when it was clear he was fine, she found herself staring at this dangerous-looking man and marveling at the fact that just a few hours ago he had been naked in her arms, in her bed…in her.

Draven's eyes locked with hers. His expression didn't change, but the green of his eyes seemed to go hot, as if he'd read her thoughts.

And as if those thoughts had the same effect on him as they'd had on her.

"It's going to be over soon," he said, still looking at her, and his voice oddly soft.

"It went well?" Kieren asked.

Draven never took his eyes off of her. "Well enough," he said.

"What went well?" Marly asked. "What did you do?"

At last he shifted his gaze, and Grace could breathe again.

"Started a ball rolling," he said.

Marly frowned. "What does that mean?"

"If it works, I'll tell you. If it doesn't, I'll keep my mouth shut and save my pride."

Marly gave him a sideways look. "Yeah, right. Like anything you do doesn't work."

Draven lifted a brow at her. She grinned.

"I've been listening to Kieren."

It was the young man's turn to look uncomfortable. "Come on, Marly," he said. "Let's get out of here for a while. Been cooped up long enough."

The girl approved his suggestion quickly, ran to get her sandals, and they headed outside.

Draven walked over to the sofa, reached down beside it and pulled up the black duffel bag. He then reversed the process she'd seen before, removing the ankle holster and the small gun it contained, then the knife in his boot. The items out of the jacket came next, and then the jacket itself came off.

He placed it all in the duffel, including the jacket, and zipped it shut. It had to have been warm with even that lightweight jacket, but he showed no sign of sweating. Nor of discomfort. That is, until he tugged his T-shirt out of his waistband as if it were too hot. The movement gave her a glimpse of the flat, hard belly she'd rested her head on this afternoon, and she was flooded with heat all over again.

Flustered, she repeated Marly's question. "What did you do?"

"I told you I was going to put an end to this."

"Yes, you did. But how? What did you mean about starting a ball rolling? What ball?"

"One that should end up at our saboteur."

Grace stifled a sigh of annoyance at his vagary. "Exactly what did you do today?"

"Feeling the need to keep track of me now?" he asked, with a lifted brow that sent a stab of hurt through her. She knew what he meant, that she was presuming on the change in their relationship. The hurt changed swiftly to anger.

"I feel," she said stiffly, "the need to know what's going on with the project I'm responsible for. As project manager, I'm asking to be kept in the loop."

"Grace," he began.

"What," she said again, "did you do today?"

He let out a compressed breath. "Made a deal with the devil."

Chapter 20

He'd really ticked her off, Draven thought. Not that he could blame her. He hadn't meant to say that, about her keeping track of him; it was simply that he wasn't used to having to account to anyone. And—somewhat to his surprise—he didn't even mind that. His question had been mostly curious. But she had obviously taken it as an accusation. And now, he had no idea what to say to alleviate the situation. But he knew he had to try. He wasn't exactly sure why, but he knew it.

"If you'd said yes, Grace, it would have been all right." *I would have liked it,* he added silently, unable yet to go that far aloud. It was hard enough to admit to himself that he liked the idea of this woman wanting to keep track of him.

"Gee, thanks," she said, her tone telling him he was still not forgiven. "A simple answer to my question, please? Without veiled references no one but you can understand?"

He was going to have to tell her, he realized. She did have

a right to know, as the project manager. And he realized with a little shock that he'd been trying to protect her by withholding the information. Not that protecting someone, especially one of Redstone's own, was unusual for him. It was just unusual for him to do it for personal reasons. And he didn't think he could deny any longer that that was what had happened with Grace.

And he had a suspicion it had been going on long before now, when he'd finally realized it.

So, he was going to have to tell her the truth. She had the right to know, and also the need to know, so she didn't inadvertently get caught up in the long row of dominoes he'd started falling today. Besides, she was going to have to be involved, if only in name as the manager of the project. He had to tell her, and he guessed she wasn't going to like that, either.

Might as well get it over with, he thought.

"I convinced *el mercader* it was in his best interest to help me stop our saboteur."

She stared at him as if he'd spoken in some strange language she'd never heard before. He felt the urge to respond to the look, to explain himself, and in rueful silence he chalked up yet another change.

"I thought he *was* our saboteur."

"I don't think so."

"Why?"

He didn't think "Too obvious" was going to fly with her. Nor would "He told me he wasn't." Yet all he had beyond that was an instinct from a gut that he didn't completely trust anymore, and he suspected that would be even less acceptable to her.

"It's my job to make those decisions."

Her gaze narrowed, as if she sensed he didn't have a concrete reason to give her. But she let it drop and went on to what obviously bothered her more.

"So you made the decision and then made a deal with a drug trafficker?"

"Made a deal with someone who's got the men and the motivation to do the job."

"A drug dealer."

"He's the tool at hand."

"The ends justify the means?"

"In this case."

She stared at him. "I can't believe this. You're cooperating with a drug dealer?"

"It's a matter of priorities."

"Priorities? That's what you call it?"

"Safety of Redstone personnel is the first priority," he quoted from the most basic philosophy Redstone was founded on.

"And dealing with some drug lord is going to guarantee that how?"

"Grace—"

"Half the reason I brought Marly out here was because a couple of her friends were getting into drugs! And now you've invited someone who deals in that evil right into our midst?"

"I didn't invite him to dinner," Draven pointed out.

That it was the wrong thing to say took only a split second to realize. And the outraged look she gave him told him this was a losing battle. And he'd already fought it longer than he ever would have with anyone but her.

"You don't have to approve, Grace."

"I just have to go along? Well, I don't think so. I'm in charge of this project, and you can just call off whatever sleazy deal you've made right now."

With a sigh, he turned to the last resort. "Do you know who has the final word on what gets done at Redstone?"

She frowned. "Josh."

He shook his head. "I do. If I tell him no, it doesn't happen."

Her mouth twisted as if she thought he was exaggerating. "You just call Josh and everything comes to a halt?"

"Yes." He saw her realize he wasn't kidding.

"I suppose you give Josh orders, too?"

"When it comes to safety, I'm his boss, yes." He looked at her steadily. "And right now, I'm your boss."

She went very still. "So you're ordering me to go along with this?"

"If I have to."

"Oh, you'll have to," Grace said, and he heard the spark of anger in her tone.

"Consider it done. Here's what's going to happen."

Grace couldn't remember when she'd been so angry. She knew a large part of it was that she felt betrayed, by the man she'd trusted enough to take to her bed.

And that man had turned back into the stoic, laconic, grim-faced man he'd been when he'd first arrived. It wasn't until now that she realized just how much he'd relaxed since then.

She told herself she didn't care, not when he'd truly made that devil's bargain. Doing anything in cooperation with the kind of slime who had nearly gotten their hooks into her daughter just went against everything she believed in. It did indeed feel like a betrayal.

She didn't even look at him as they made their way to the airstrip site, where the paving work had restarted. She didn't know if she could ever really look at him again. Didn't know if she wanted to. And now when she thought about that afternoon they'd spent together, she felt only a chilling sense of loss.

That will teach you, she thought, although she wasn't

sure what exactly the lesson was supposed to be. She told herself to look upon it as a momentary aberration and get on with business.

One of the crew approached her as soon as she got over to the trucks. "Ms. O'Conner?" one of them said. "Is it true? About Chuck dying?"

Grace still didn't look at Draven. She drew in a deep breath. She'd known this was going to be hard, hated having to do it, but she had no choice.

"I'm afraid so," she said. "Word came in this morning."

"Damn," the man said.

"Yes," she agreed.

He turned and walked back to the rest of the crew, and she could almost see the confirmation spread. Apprehension on faces turned to shock and sorrow, and Grace hated every second of it.

When, at Draven's direction, she drove them into town for the mail, she found the news had already traveled. Yvette in the post office window greeted her with condolences, then asked, "Is it true that your company has sent in their own police force, and they'll be here tomorrow?"

Grace blinked. "Well, I wouldn't call it a police force," she began.

"No," Draven agreed, the first time he'd spoken since they'd left the site. "They don't have to obey the rules the police do. They don't have to be nice, call you a lawyer or account for any injuries you might sustain. So they're more effective."

The woman's eyes widened. Grace barely kept hers from doing the same at the way he was exaggerating. At least, she thought he was exaggerating. Perhaps, all things considered, she was being too generous.

She tried to fight down the bitterness that threatened to well up inside her. Throughout everything she'd managed for the most part not to become bitter, and wasn't sure why it was so close now. Perhaps because this time it was her own bad judgment that had brought her to this.

"Is it true they will be here to avenge this death?" Yvette asked, her eyes still wide.

"We are a family," Draven said with a shrug, as if that answered the question.

Grace couldn't think of a thing to say to him as they left the small grocery and headed down the street. When they made a stop in the general store, Mr. Ayuso also offered his condolences on Chuck's death.

"And that girl of yours," he added to Grace, "she's all right. Apologized for what she did, and paid me back. She can come back in, if she wants."

It was all Grace could do not to look at Draven, the architect of that particular transformation. She didn't want to look at him, or even think about it, how a man who could do that, who could care enough to think of a way to wake up a child on the edge of trouble, could turn around and make a pact with a drug dealer.

After a few more stops it became clear that the news of Chuck's death was a hot topic. As, it appeared, was the imminent arrival of a full force of Redstone security, which seemed in most islanders' minds to be tantamount to an invading army bound by no rules.

They were back in the truck, Draven behind the wheel—like so many other things in the past few hours, he'd given her no option about that—when his cell phone rang. He flipped it open and spoke into the receiver.

"Draven." A pause while he listened. "Is that the only movement?" Another pause. "Anyone with him?" And then, finally, "I'll take it. Have your guy stand by."

He disconnected and closed the phone, tossing it on the seat beside him. "We think we've got him."

She knew it should have been that news that had the most impact, but instead it was that "we."

"That was him? *El mercader?*"

Draven eyed her warily for a moment before nodding. She suppressed a shiver.

"Go back in the store. I'll call Buckley. He can pick you up there."

She was already very tired of taking his orders. "Why?"

"Grace, I've got to go."

"Before he gets away?" She knew she was right when she saw the split-second flicker in his gaze. "Then go."

"Not with you."

She tried not to be insulted, knowing he was simply trying to protect her. That had never stopped, despite her fury with him. She also didn't relish the idea of being anywhere near *el mercader* or his men. But neither did she relish the idea of sitting and waiting like a good little girl to see if Draven came back alive.

Not, she admitted ruefully, that she wouldn't like to murder him right now. But she wanted to reserve that pleasure for herself.

Besides, if the man behind all this had really been found, she wanted to know who he was. And she wanted to look him in the eye and make him see he hadn't won.

"You can sit here and argue with me some more and miss your chance," she said cheerfully. "Or you can try to force me out of the truck, which while I won't deny you'll be able to do it, I promise it will take long enough for you to miss your chance. Or you can shut up and drive."

She expected him to yell, to swear, to do anything but what he did.

"Touché," he said softly.

And then he put the truck in gear and they started to move. Before she was over her surprise at that, he shocked her again, reaching beneath the driver's seat and pulling out the small handgun she'd seen him strap to his ankle before and handing it to her.

"I hope you've kept up," he said.

She stared at the gun in her hand, felt the compact, heavy weight of it. As per Josh's orders, any of his people who went to some of the less civilized or peaceful parts of the world knew how to defend themselves, so she had been through the standard firearms course Redstone provided. She'd done better with rifles than pistols, but she'd passed.

Of course, that had been years ago. She told herself that didn't matter; she wasn't going to have to put every round in the ten ring as the instructor had wanted then.

"It's a revolver," she said, remembering what the Redstone instructor, a former SWAT cop, had told her all that time ago. "Point and shoot."

"Pretty much," Draven agreed.

She gave him a sideways glance. For some reason the day she'd first arrived in Turkey came to mind. She remembered meeting Redstone point man Noah Rider there. Rider had been classically chiseled. Draven was scarred and rugged. Rider had been open and amusing. Draven was taciturn and solemn.

Yet it was Draven who stirred her pulse, while Rider had left her aesthetically appreciative, but unmoved.

So is that lousy taste, or just lousy judgment? she wondered to herself.

Or perhaps it was simply that Rider radiated contentment, especially when the subject of his wife, Paige, arose.

Draven started issuing orders as he drove. "You stay in the truck. In the driver's seat. You shoot only to protect yourself. If anything goes wrong, or you hear shots, you get the hell out. Get back to the site and to Buckley. Got it?"

"Yes, sir," she said.

He shot her a sharp glance, but she had kept her voice carefully neutral and didn't look at him now. She didn't dare look at him, not after the image he'd called up in her mind of her sitting here wondering which end of those shots he'd been on.

"I mean it, Grace."

"I never thought you didn't."

He went silent again. They went north through the rest of the small town, then, to her surprise, past the clinic that was on the outskirts. They made a turn just beyond that and started up the slight hill that rose above the village. It was thick with acacia trees and hibiscus run wild as undergrowth, and would make for a great hiding place if you needed one.

He stopped short of the top, where the gravel road ended. Quickly and efficiently, even on the narrow road, he turned the truck around so it was facing downhill and out. For her, she realized with a sinking feeling, in case she had to run.

"If you hear a car coming down," he said, "get out and take cover off the road. Don't wait to think about it."

Her brows furrowed, but she nodded. When he got out of the truck, she slid over behind the wheel. He nodded, then turned to head toward the junglelike hillside.

Then he turned back.

"Grace?"

She looked up.

"It had to stop. This was the quickest way."

She took in a deep breath. She sensed that this was an exception for him. That John Draven didn't waste breath explaining himself. And she wondered why he'd felt compelled to do it now. It wasn't an apology, yet that was the undertone in his voice.

And then he was gone, so quickly she couldn't quite believe it. Almost instantly he was out of sight in the brush, and she couldn't even see a leaf moving to mark his passage.

She looked around, something tickling the edges of her memory. She thought she might have been up here before, but she couldn't be sure. The road and the surroundings looked familiar, but her memory was telling her it had been different.

It had been dark, she suddenly realized. That's why she hadn't been sure if this had been the same road. But she was almost positive now, and—

The sound of a vehicle approaching from farther up the hill cut off her thoughts. For a brief moment she simply sat there, listening, making sure she was really hearing it. And then Draven's order played through her head.

Get out. Don't think, get out.

She scrambled across the seat to the passenger door, yanked it open and slid to the ground. The engine sound was closer, as if it were rounding the curve just beyond the truck.

And it was coming fast.

She felt a little foolish—what if it was just some resident or tourist—but the fierceness of Draven's warning echoed in her ears, and she dove for the shelter of the huge, orange-flowered hibiscus that was the closest to the side of the road.

She crouched down, peering back through the glossy leaves, looking up toward the curve where anything coming down the road would come around the hill. She caught a glimpse of something long and white and shiny moving fast. Far too fast for the road.

It slammed into the parked truck.

The wrenching, nerve-shattering noise of the impact made her cry out instinctively. She smothered the sound, although she doubted anyone could have heard anything over the noise of the crash. The big white car hit with such force the pickup skewed sideways, and she flinched back as it seemed to be coming right at her.

The echoes of the crash finally seemed to stop, and the

only thing she heard was the slight tinkle of shattered glass falling, and the drip of something liquid. Certain someone had to have been hurt, she stood up. As she did she caught sight of the side of the truck. The driver's door, where she had been sitting, was demolished. The entire truck had buckled on that side, and she was reasonably sure if she had stayed there she would have been badly hurt or even killed.

She heard somebody swearing, and what sounded like a woman crying. The presence of the female decided her, and she scrambled back to the road and ran toward the wreck. She got there just as the driver managed to force open his door, obviously also buckled by the impact.

Her relief that the man was moving, and apparently all right, was quickly overtaken by shock.

It was Mayor Remington.

She wasn't surprised, since she'd just realized this was the road they'd driven the night he had thrown the party at his house to welcome Redstone to the island. His luxurious home was the last one at the top of the hill.

Oh, boy, Redstone's not going to like this, she thought. *We've destroyed the mayor's fancy car.*

The woman she'd heard wasn't getting out. Seeing that the mayor, who apparently hadn't seen her yet, was up and moving, she instead ran to the other side of the car. In the passenger seat was the source of the weeping she'd heard, not a woman but a girl, who looked even younger than Marly. Grace didn't see any immediate signs of injury, but since she hadn't gotten out of the car she had to think something was wrong.

Then the girl seemed to realize she was there. She looked up at Grace, her dark eyes wide and full of tears, and something else, some wilder thing Grace couldn't put a name to.

"Please," the girl gulped out.

"Ms. O'Conner?"

The mayor's voice made her straighten and look over at him. "Are you all right?" she asked him.

"I think so," he said, watching her in an oddly intent way. "What are you doing here?"

This wasn't the time to explain, especially since she didn't really have the answer.

"I think your passenger may be hurt," she said, bending back down to look at the girl. "We'd better call for help."

"I don't think so."

There was something different about his voice, very different than the jovial man who had welcomed her here.

"But she may need—"

Grace's words stopped abruptly. She'd just seen the reason the girl hadn't gotten out of the wrecked car.

She was tied to the seat.

Grace looked across the car roof at Mayor Remington in shock. And got an even bigger shock.

He was pointing a gun at her.

Chapter 21

Grace.

Draven had never felt anything like the jolt of horror that stabbed through him like a sizzling poker when he heard the crash.

He had just put his cell phone back in his pocket after *el mercader* had called again, saying their man was on the move. Mere seconds later he'd heard the vehicle on the road.

He'd known immediately it was traveling too fast. It either wouldn't make the curve, or if it did it would be because the driver likely stayed so tight to the edge he couldn't help but hit the truck.

Even as he thought it, the sound of the impact ripped through the tropical air.

Instantly he spun around and reversed his course. He couldn't be sure this was their ultimate quarry, but he didn't care. There was only one vehicle that whoever it was could have hit, and that was all that mattered.

For the first time in his life his work fell completely off the radar. Nothing was in his mind but getting back to Grace. Thoughts of silence, caution, strategy and reconnaissance vanished as he fought his way back to the road where he'd left the truck.

And the woman he suddenly and belatedly realized he didn't want to leave behind. Ever.

Only when he got within earshot did he slow enough to approach silently. When he reached the edge of the brush he saw a scene out of his worst nightmare. The mangled remains of the truck and the mayor's car sat half off the road, obviously pushed by the force of the collision. His gaze zeroed in on the driver's seat where he'd left Grace; if she'd been there, she was surely dead.

And then, after a moment when he couldn't breathe, his focus widened. He took in the entire scene. Including Grace, alive and out of the truck. He could breathe again.

She was on the far side of the wrecked car. The mayor was on the near side. And he was holding a chrome revolver pointed across the crumpled roof at Grace.

Draven had only a split second to assess. Grace was looking at something inside the car, possibly a passenger. Given what he'd just learned, Draven thought he had an idea who that passenger might be. But Grace wasn't bent down far enough to be out of any line of fire, his or Remington's. Draven's mind raced, looking for the answer.

"Stop it, bitch!" Remington yelled across the car at her, obviously unaware of Draven's presence.

Grace ignored him, and ignored the weapon trained on her. She continued to work on something inside the car, from here Draven couldn't tell what.

But Remington was starting to lose it. The gun waved wildly, and Draven thought he was just crazy enough to fire it by accident. He dodged behind the remains of the truck.

Headed for the front. Rounded it, which put him on a straight line with his target.

At the last second, he slammed his fist down on the bent hood of the truck. The hollow, metallic thud made Grace's head snap upward.

More important, it startled Remington. And he turned.

The instant the weapon was no longer trained on Grace, Draven launched himself.

He hit the man at the waist. The impetus sent him sprawling backward. They hit the ground together. Draven made sure his shoulder dug deep, heard the grunt and whoosh of air escaping Remington's lungs. At the same time he assessed. Calculated with the swiftness of long experience what he was dealing with.

The man was soft.

But it didn't take strength to fire the pistol. And Grace was still vulnerable. A wild shot could be disastrous.

The gun was the goal.

Remington realized that, too. He twisted, trying to bring the gun to bear. Draven shifted, trying to get leverage. Remington grunted, twisted.

The gun went off.

Draven felt the familiar sharp burn and sting of a bullet leaving a gouge on his right arm. Swiftly he calculated. Angle, trajectory. Decided Grace should have been safe. Rolled, until he had the man pinned. He clamped a hand over Remington's. Tightened his fingers. The man swore. Draven slid a finger and his thumb forward, gripping the cylinder so it couldn't rotate.

Remington began to flail, striking out wildly with his free left hand. He landed some glancing blows, nothing Draven couldn't ignore. At least, until he managed to squarely hit the spot where the bullet had grazed Draven's arm.

Draven winced, his jaw tightening. He turned the concentration he'd developed early in his life onto one thing: keeping his hold on the gun. He poured every bit of strength he could into his grip. He envisioned pushing Remington's fingers through the gunmetal. The man pulled desperately, trying to break free of the relentless squeeze.

In his gyrations Remington finally twisted so that Draven could see his eyes. He fixed his gaze, concentrating. Never wavering. He saw the fear dawn, then spread across Remington's face. He'd never been certain what it was about him that did it, only that it happened.

In the moment when Remington gave up, Draven became aware that someone was beside him. He flicked a glance upward.

Grace. The small weapon he'd given her in her hands, aimed and ready to fire.

He had to force himself to keep his mind on the job at hand, and even when he looked back at Remington, it was the image of Grace on guard at his side that was uppermost in his mind.

As Draven wrested the gun away from the now exhausted Remington Grace lowered her arms, thankful she hadn't had to shoot. Her gaze fastened on Draven's right arm, just below the shoulder.

"You're bleeding," she said.

"I imagine so."

"We need to get you to the clinic."

"I'm fine."

Grace grimaced. "Be stubborn, then. But there's a girl in the car, and I think she's hurt, too."

"Probably more than you know," Draven said grimly. "We'll get her to the clinic, and then we can have the pleasure of turning the former mayor here over to Sergeant Espinoza."

Remington muttered something under his breath. Grace

looked at him, then at Draven. "What do you mean, more than I know?"

Draven looked at Remington, who at the moment was looking like the cockroach he was. "He was probably going to deliver her. To a buyer."

Grace's brow furrowed. "What?"

"Seems the mayor had a lucrative little sideline going. Little girls for men with sick tastes. He's running because he heard the rumor *el mercader* started that he himself was bailing out because Redstone was sending an army for revenge."

"Little girls?" Grace gasped, her eyes widening.

"That's why he didn't want the airstrip built, or Redstone here. He thought it would interfere with his sex trade."

She glanced back at the car, where the girl still sat. The girl who was not much older than her own precious child. Then she looked back at Remington.

"Is this true?"

He called her a name in Spanish. She didn't recognize it, but with his tone that was hardly necessary. And Draven's reaction—placing his foot atop the man's throat and telling him if he spoke once more he would never speak again—just made it clearer.

"My God," Grace whispered, staring at the man on the ground.

She tried to wrap her mind around the idea, but she just couldn't. At least, not yet, while the shock was fresh. She willingly held her small gun on the man she'd thought of as, if not a friend, at least a decent person, while Draven checked the vehicles. Her aim was rock steady as she looked at him.

Remington looked up at her assessingly. It didn't take Draven's training or experience to guess what he was thinking.

"If you think I'd hesitate to rid the world of you, you're

very mistaken," she said softly. The look faded from eyes that now held only fear.

Draven paused and looked back, and his eyes met hers. The slight nod and even slighter smile he gave her felt as if he'd saluted. In a way she supposed he had.

He checked the truck first, but that didn't take long. She hadn't thought it would move on its own, not with the engine twisted sideways as it was. Then he went to the white sedan. He spent more time there, and it took her a few glances—all she would risk while guarding this subhuman—to realize he was searching it. Then he popped the trunk open—one of the few unbent areas on the car—looked inside, then walked back toward them.

"Neither one is drivable," he said.

"Now what?" Grace asked. "That poor child needs to be checked, and her parents contacted. She's terrified."

Draven didn't take long to think about it. "Are you all right with Marly staying with Nick until you get back?"

"Fine," she said, only realizing then that it was actually over.

He pulled out his cell, called Buckley and told him to leave Marly with Nick and meet them here ASAP. Then he called Sergeant Espinoza, told him where they were and to come and take custody of Remington. Then he walked over to the man and yanked him up on his feet. He propelled him toward the back of the car, and to Grace's surprise pushed him into the trunk.

Remington started to scream.

"I suggest you save some of that wind to let Sergeant Espinoza know you're in there when he gets here," Draven suggested mildly.

"Or not," Grace said.

Draven looked at her. "Feeling a bit bloodthirsty?"

"Yes," she said simply.

One corner of his mouth shot upward in a lopsided grin that made her pulse jam into overdrive. She hated that she couldn't control her response to him, even when she was so angry about what he'd done.

And now that the reason he'd come here was past, she didn't know what was going to happen.

He slammed the trunk closed.

"Now we can go tell Chuck he's alive again," Draven said.

The plan she had helped carry out had worked.

Grace sat in a chair in the small waiting area of the clinic, looking shell-shocked and a little green. The doctor had confirmed their worst fears: the twelve-year-old girl they had rescued had already been molested. She had no permanent physical injuries, but Draven doubted she would ever be completely normal again. St. John had managed to track down her family over on mainland Belize, and a Redstone escort would have them here before the end of the day.

He wasn't sure he'd be welcome, but he found he couldn't simply stand here and watch her shiver. He went over and crouched beside her chair.

"Grace," he began.

She looked up. "I went to his house. I took *Marly* to his house. I thought he was nice, for spending so much time with her, talking to her."

"You had no way of knowing."

"How did you know?"

"I suspected him because he was so insistent it had to be *el mercader.* Wouldn't listen to any other possibility."

She looked thoughtful and then, as if remembering, she nodded slowly. *"El mercader,"* she muttered, avoiding his eyes, and he knew he was still in trouble.

"He's the one who found out about the girls. He'd known

Remington was up to something, but wasn't sure what. He—" Draven stopped as the clinic door opened and a man walked in. "He's here," he ended with a sigh, thinking there was no way this could be good for him.

Grace's head snapped up, and she stared at the tall, graceful man who walked toward them. He came to a halt beside Draven, nodded, and then looked at Grace.

"Ms. O'Conner," he said, inclining his head.

She stood up, and faced *el mercader* straight on. "I'm afraid I'm not comfortable talking to people who hide behind nicknames."

Draven blinked as she said almost exactly what he had. *El mercader's* glance flicked from her to Draven and back, apparent amusement gleaming in his eyes.

"Oh?"

"You did the right thing on this," she admitted, "and for that I'm thankful."

"But on everything else I'm out in the cold," *el mercader* said.

"Your choice," she said, her voice stiff and formal.

"Not really," he said, an unmistakable tone of irony in his voice. He looked at Draven. "The girl?"

"She'll be all right. Physically."

"Are you certain you don't want me to take care of our illustrious mayor?"

Draven grimaced. "No," he said honestly. "But it's Redstone policy to turn criminals over to authorities."

"Too bad," *el mercader* said. He glanced at Grace again. "A pleasure, Ms. O'Conner. For one of us, anyway."

He turned as if to go.

"Don't forget our agreement," Draven said.

El mercader turned back. "I'm not likely to. I've done some investigating, and I'm fully aware of your reputation."

Draven nodded, and *el mercader* started for the door. His hand on the handle, he looked back over his shoulder.

"Ms. O'Conner?"

She looked at him.

"Quinn Pedragon," he said.

She blinked in surprise at the soft pronouncement of the name. Draven was a little surprised himself.

"If you take the opportunity to go straight," he said, "contact me."

The man at the door looked startled, then he chuckled. "If that should happen, I will."

And then he was gone.

Slowly she turned to look at Draven. He braced himself inwardly, wondering how he'd let himself get to the point that this woman had such power that she could make him bleed just by disapproving.

"What agreement?"

It was pointless to dissemble, he thought. She couldn't get any angrier with him than she already was.

"That by the time Redstone finishes building the resort, he and his operation will be gone."

"Oh." She glanced at the door again. "Do you think he will keep his word?"

"I do now, yes."

She looked back at him. "Why now?"

"Because now I know his name. And he knows it."

"You don't think it was an alias."

"No."

Not the way he looked at you, he added silently, trying to quash the way that had made him feel. At first he hadn't recognized the feeling that had flashed up in him at *el mercader's*—Quinn Pedragon's—frank appreciation. When he did realize it was jealousy, he had to admit for the first time just how much trouble he was in. And hearing her speak to him in that cool, detached tone was somehow worse than any physical pain he'd ever felt.

There was only one thing he could think of to do. And all the way back to the site he tried to wrap his mind around the fact that that one thing was to run.

Chapter 22

Grace found it nearly impossible to let go of her daughter, and did so only when the girl finally protested that she couldn't breathe.

It had taken Grace a while to think beyond the horror that innocent child, the child they'd returned to weeping, grateful parents yesterday, had gone through. To think beyond that victim to others. The only thing that had made it bearable was the knowledge of those that had been saved, those children Remington would never get his hands on.

Then she had finally had to face the grim reality that Marly could have been one of them.

And it was then that she belatedly understood Draven's talk of priorities. The thought of her daughter as a target of such a sick, twisted mind made her shiver with a combination of fear and outrage and fury that had her shaking every time she thought of it. And she knew that she would have done far worse than deal with a man like Quinn Pedragon to get her back.

She owed Draven an apology. A long and sincere one. She stood up, and slipped on the one shoe she'd shed for coolness when she'd gotten back to the motor home.

"Where are you going?" Marly asked, in a tone that nearly echoed Grace's own concerned one. Marly had been more upset than she'd let on about the explosion, and seemed to have finally realized how close she had come to being motherless.

"I need to find…Mr. Draven," Grace said. *John. Johnny,* she thought. "I have to tell him something."

Marly drew back, her brows furrowed. "But he's gone."

"What?"

"He left. This morning, early. One of the Nunez brothers picked him up."

"He left?" Grace was stunned. "Without even saying goodbye?"

"He said goodbye to me," Marly said, watching her mother so closely Grace wondered what had been said during that goodbye.

"I see." Despite her efforts, the hurt she was feeling seeped into her voice.

"Mom," Marly said, sounding for all the world like a parent pointing out something obvious to a child, "what did you expect? You were so mad at him we could all see it. Why would he hang around?"

Grace stared at her child, wondering at the vivid flash of adult perception.

"Face it, Mom," Marly said. "You blew it."

Grace blinked. "Blew…what?"

"Come on," Marly said with teenaged disgust. "Do you think I'm stupid? I know you were hot for each other." Grace gaped at the girl, who rolled her eyes. "Puh-leeze," she said. "Even Kieren noticed."

Recovering slightly, Grace swallowed and asked, "And if that was true, how would you feel about it?"

"You mean if you like, got married or something?" She shrugged one shoulder in an almost eerie imitation of Draven's habit. "It'd be cool, I think. We could get along, mostly. I could tell my friends I've got a real tough guy for a stepdad."

"You'd like it?" Grace was so stunned she couldn't quite take in what she was hearing.

Marly shrugged again, and then lowered her eyes. With a visible amount of embarrassment she said, "I know I messed things up for you. I heard him tell you he couldn't…deal with me. But I changed, didn't I? I paid back old Mr. Ayuso, and I worked hard, and—"

"Yes, you did." Grace was even more shocked to hear that this was at least part of the reason for Marly's turnaround. For a moment she just sat there, trying to process everything. But there was just too much, between these revelations, what had happened, and on top of it all the realization that she had let go the first man she'd really felt anything for in years.

Felt anything? Face it, you love him. You love him, and you drove him away.

Her first instinct was to go after him. She could call, say he'd forgotten something and ask where he'd gone. Or she could—

A knock on the door sent her heart hammering again. He'd come back!

When she yanked open the door to see Nick standing there, it was a great effort not to let her disappointment show in her face.

"Sorry," Nick said, "but there's a problem. The roller we rented broke down, and the rental outfit says they can't get here for two days."

"I'll handle it," she said automatically.

"And there's some environmental guy here, wants to know when we're going to get the native plants back in place."

Grace sighed. There was just too much to do right now, she couldn't afford to leave. She wouldn't do that to Josh, or to Redstone.

"I'll see him."

Wearily she pulled on her shoe and went back to work.

Grace knew she was probably exhausted, but she was too numb to feel it. In a final, hard push they'd finished the airstrip two days ago. Shortly after she filed that report, Redstone headquarters sent word to expect Josh himself to take a look.

She put the crew to work finishing the terminal, now obviously behind schedule because of the explosion. She'd gotten a copy of the Redstone report on the incident, that explained about bomb materials found in the garage of Remington's home, and that he'd paid a local who'd been making a delivery to the site to plant it, just as he had with the other incidents.

She also saw the report that the late-night prowler that had tripped the alarm was in fact one of Pedragon's men, starting his own investigation because of the increasing heat suspicion was casting on them.

The fact that all the reports were signed "John Draven," in a bold, compact hand, was something she tried to ignore. Unsuccessfully, as a sick feeling rose in her, bringing her near to desperation.

She was sitting in the shade of the motor home's awning, trying futilely to think about something else, anything else, when the sound of a jet engine from above dragged her out of her wallow of misery. She looked up and saw the familiar colors of red and slate gray. Josh Redstone had obviously arrived.

Grateful for the distraction, Grace got up as the sleek little jet banked on approach. She wondered if Tess Machado was at the controls; she hadn't seen Tess in a while, and she always enjoyed talking to her.

She realized suddenly she was still wearing the grubby clothes she'd had on when she'd done her final inspection of the charred debris that had been cleared from the explosion site. Josh didn't expect anybody to dress up for him, but she thought the least she could do was be clean. Josh would likely stop to talk to the crew anyway, that was his way. So she had a few minutes.

She dashed inside and washed her face and hands, changed into clean khakis and a light blue shirt, put on clean socks and her cleanest sneakers, and ran a brush through her wind-tousled hair. Then she started toward the airfield.

When she arrived she was startled to see Josh in apparently deep conversation, not with the crew but with Marly. Josh saw her coming, smiled and waved. But Marly reacted very strangely, almost guiltily jumping back and avoiding looking at her mother.

Josh enveloped Grace in a hug, his usual greeting for the people who'd been with him any length of time.

"Looks great," he said.

She smiled up at the lean, gray-eyed man. "Well, except for the terminal."

He waved a hand as if the delay meant nothing. "You'll have more help here in another day or so. It'll get done."

She hadn't asked for help, but she wasn't about to turn it down. She had a record of bringing projects in on time, and she didn't want to blow it on this first one after the earthquake.

"The strip is as smooth as a quarter horse's coat in the summertime." Josh's drawl was exaggerated, like it usually was when he tossed out one of those down-home homilies. She wondered how many people had been lured into thinking he was stupid or slow because of that drawl.

And then left in shock when they found out just how quick and sharp the mind behind that lazy drawl was, Grace thought with pride.

"Should I go pack?" Marly asked.

"Good idea," Josh said.

Grace frowned. "Pack? For what?"

"We're going home," Marly said, sounding excited.

Grace thought in that moment that if she got hit with one more jolt she was going to crawl into a hole.

"Just for a visit," Marly said. "We'll be back in a week, but I'll get to see my friends."

So that's what they were plotting, Grace thought.

She had thought the girl had gotten to liking it here—especially after Kieren's arrival—but apparently she was still missing home. Grace didn't like the thought that Marly might have manipulated her boss into offering this ride, but she was so excited Grace couldn't bring herself to deny her. Besides, she doubted anyone successfully manipulated Josh Redstone into anything he wasn't already willing to do.

She didn't want to be gone from the project, but she could hardly let Marly go alone. She supposed she could call Aunt Charlotte, but she'd been ill, and it was a bit much to—

"It's all right, Grace," Josh said. "Nick can keep things going for a week."

She smiled ruefully. "Am I that transparent?"

"'Fraid so," Josh said with a grin. "Go pack some things. I want to take off ASAP."

Grace knew an order when she heard one. After returning to the motor home and putting some things in a bag, Grace walked back to the strip with Marly at her heels.

"You didn't come all the way here just for this, did you?" she asked Josh.

"Nah. I wanted some hours at the controls," he said, indicating the sleek plane on the strip, his own Hawk IV.

"It's cool looking," Marly said.

Josh looked at the girl. "I need a copilot. Interested?"

Marly's eyes got bigger than Grace had ever seen them. "I don't know how to fly!"

"Then it's time you learned," Josh said.

Marly turned stunned but excited eyes on Grace. "Mom?"

"No one better to learn from," she said.

"Wow!"

The girl darted up the steps into the plane. "Right seat!" Josh called out after her. Bare seconds later Grace saw her daughter through the cockpit window.

Josh took her bag for her, and she started up the steps. Josh walked up behind her, and when they stepped into the plane he turned and hit the button that brought up the steps and closed the door. Once the brilliant tropical sun was blocked, Grace could see the inside of the Redstone jet. She'd been flown here on a Hawk III, and had thought it incredible. This was even more so, with polished woods, gleaming fixtures and the rich upholstery on the seating, more like a living room than a plane.

That was all she saw. Because at the far end of the passenger compartment, sitting at a polished, light burl wood table beside a window, was a man.

Draven.

"Work it out," Josh ordered before turning to vanish into the cockpit.

For a long, strained moment Grace simply looked at him. Then she heard the jets fire as Josh started them.

"You'd better sit down and strap in," Draven said.

He nodded at the seat across from him. For a moment she considered taking a seat at the opposite end of the cabin, but realized it would be childish. So she sucked in a breath and sat down opposite him.

"I—"

"I—"

They started simultaneously, then both stopped. Draven gestured her to go ahead.

"I'm sorry," she said. "I didn't understand. But the minute I thought about Marly in that pervert's hands, I knew what you meant about priorities. I was wrong. You were right. You did what was necessary."

She thought she saw surprise flicker across his face. "What? No one's ever apologized to you before?"

"Most often," he said mildly, "no one has the nerve to do anything that would bring on the need to apologize to me."

It wasn't said with arrogance, but was a simple statement of fact. And she supposed it was true.

"Haven't dealt with a lot of mothers?"

His mouth quirked. "Only my own. And I was usually the one apologizing to her."

He didn't seem angry. In fact, he seemed almost amused. Which surprised her. And encouraged her. Unless of course he'd simply decided she was only worth laughing at for her naiveté.

Nervous at that idea, her fingers began to trace circles on the glossy tabletop.

"You deal in ugliness so often," she said softly. "How do you stay sane?"

And suddenly the amusement was gone. He leaned forward. Reached out. Put his hand over hers, stopping her fingers. And her breath. She stared at the table as if her life depended on memorizing the rich grain of the wood. And then she felt his other hand gently lift her chin, making her look at him. And there was an intensity in his green eyes she'd never seen before.

"Because," he said, just as softly, "sometimes, if I'm lucky, there's also beauty. And goodness. And courage."

The sweet gentleness of those words from this tough,

fierce man rocked her to the core. She couldn't think at all, no words, no response came to her. So she simply stared at him, drinking in the expression on his face, in his eyes, before she even had a name for what was there.

"I'm no prize, Grace. I've got a lot of rough edges." He took in an audible breath. "I never thought there could be a woman tough enough to handle what I do and the life it demands."

"I've never let difficulties stop me," she said, aware of the breathy tone of her voice, but unable to stop it.

"I know." He hesitated, then went on. "I talked to Marly. She's okay with it. With…us. And she promised not to be such a…pain, if we promised to listen to her."

Us. We.

Grace thought she'd never heard anything so wonderful as those simple two-letter words.

Draven swallowed as if his throat were tight. And Grace realized with a little shock that he, too, was nervous.

"I've never done this. I don't… I can't… This romantic thing…"

The thought of Draven nervous, and about this, somehow gave her the last bit of courage she needed.

"Do you want to know what's romantic to me?" she asked. "It's a man who does things to make your life easier. It's a man who fixes things so you don't have to. A man who doesn't need to be waited on, who doesn't expect me to be something I'm not. Or not be what I am. *That's* romantic."

His expression changed as she spoke, the nervous edge disappearing from his voice. And slowly, he began to smile.

"I can do that," he said when she stopped.

"I know," she said.

It wasn't until much later, after they'd worked out the details, that he groaned out load as some unexpected thought obviously hit him.

"What?" Grace asked, still a little stunned at how much thought he'd put into a future for them. The three of them.

"I just realized," he said as if the thought were a painful one. "We're going to be stuck with a Redstone wedding."

She blinked. "Redstone weddings are...different?"

"Redstone weddings," he intoned gloomily, "are overwhelming."

Grace laughed. She couldn't help herself. "I'll protect you," she joked.

Draven went very still, and the look that came over his face then was one of wonder. "And you know something?" he said softly. "I'll let you."

And Grace knew then that the legendary John Draven, the man she would soon tie herself to forever, had just done the most heroic thing of his life.

* * * * *

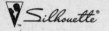

If you enjoyed what you just read,
then we've got an offer you can't resist!

Take 2 bestselling love stories FREE!

Plus get a FREE surprise gift!

Clip this page and mail it to Silhouette Reader Service™

IN U.S.A.
3010 Walden Ave.
P.O. Box 1867
Buffalo, N.Y. 14240-1867

IN CANADA
P.O. Box 609
Fort Erie, Ontario
L2A 5X3

YES! Please send me 2 free Silhouette Intimate Moments® novels and my free surprise gift. After receiving them, if I don't wish to receive anymore, I can return the shipping statement marked cancel. If I don't cancel, I will receive 6 brand-new novels every month, before they're available in stores! In the U.S.A., bill me at the bargain price of $4.24 plus 25¢ shipping and handling per book and applicable sales tax, if any*. In Canada, bill me at the bargain price of $4.99 plus 25¢ shipping and handling per book and applicable taxes**. That's the complete price and a savings of at least 10% off the cover prices—what a great deal! I understand that accepting the 2 free books and gift places me under no obligation ever to buy any books. I can always return a shipment and cancel at any time. Even if I never buy another book from Silhouette, the 2 free books and gift are mine to keep forever.

245 SDN DZ9A
345 SDN DZ9C

Name*	(PLEASE PRINT)	
Address		Apt.#
City	State/Prov.	Zip/Postal Code

Not valid to current Silhouette Intimate Moments® subscribers.

Want to try two free books from another series?
Call 1-800-873-8635 or visit www.morefreebooks.com.

 * Terms and prices subject to change without notice. Sales tax applicable in N.Y.
 ** Canadian residents will be charged applicable provincial taxes and GST.
   All orders subject to approval. Offer limited to one per household].
   ® are registered trademarks owned and used by the trademark owner or its licensee.

INMOM04R   ©2004 Harlequin Enterprises Limited

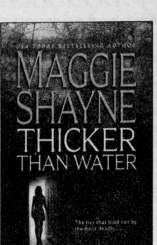

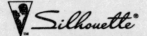

COMING NEXT MONTH